THE ELECTRIC KID

A Melanie Kroupa Book

THE ELECTRIC KID

BY GARRY KILWORTH

Orchard Books
New York

Orchard Books
95 Madison Avenue
New York, NY 10016

Manufactured in the United States of America
Book design by Chris Hammill Paul

10 9 8 7 6 5 4 3 2 1

The text of this book is set in 12½ point Janson.

Library of Congress Cataloging-in-Publication Data

Kilworth, Garry.
    The electric kid / by Garry Kilworth.—1st American ed.
        p.   cm.
    "First published in Great Britain in 1994 by Transworld
Publishers"—Verso t.p.
    "A Melanie Kroupa book"—Half title.
    Summary: Set in the year 2061, two children support
themselves in a city dump and are pressed into the service of
the criminal underworld until their unique talents foster their
escape.
    ISBN 0-531-09486-3.—ISBN 0-531-08786-7 (lib. bdg.)
    [1. Ragpickers—Fiction. 2. Homeless persons—Fiction.]
I. Title.
PZ7.K5595E1   1995
[Fic]—dc20   95-6030

*This book is dedicated to the kids
who live on the rubbish dumps of Manila.*

1

Hey, Hotwire, I think I hear something!" whispered Blindboy.

One of the other dump kids instinctively looked across at us. He hadn't heard Blindboy, but you get to sense things on the dump. When someone happens on a find, they might start to move differently, or they might stand in a certain way—it's not something you can help doing—and the rest of the kids know that something's going on.

The boy's name was Buzzard and he was a lot bigger than me. Even though I wear these grown-up–sized overalls, I have to roll the sleeves and legs up. Blindboy's even smaller than me, because he's only eleven and I'm two years older than him.

"Hotwire! You find something, girl?" Buzzard shouted to me.

"Nah," I yelled back. "Blindboy gets excited about a few crusts of bread these days."

If the big kid thought we'd made a find, he'd rush over and dig it out himself. We've got this sort of rule on the dump that things aren't yours until you've dug them up and you're holding them in your hand. So you have to do everything in secret.

"Okay," I whispered to Blindboy, "when he looks away again, we'll start."

Me and Blindboy, we've done the dumps together for three years now, since October 2058. Before that we were street kids, and before that . . . Well, I don't know about Blindboy, but I had a dad to look after me, till he died in a skidder crash.

Anyway we live in these really yerky tents made of dirty polyethylene. Polyethylene's better than rags, which let in the wet, even though the rats run over it at night. Their scratchy little claws can keep you awake at first.

Nowadays the rats don't bother me too much, unless they start a fight right there on top of the tent; then I get mad at them and chase them with a stick. You can't sleep through a rat fight no matter how long you've lived here. They squeak and yell so loud it pierces you through to your eyeballs.

So me and Blindboy live right here on the biggest dump of all. It has mountains of trash covering a square klick, a whole square kilometer. There's all sorts of stuff, from slime food to garbage to decent junk like busted home computers. If you're a dump kid, you're one of hundreds, and you have to live on the top of the tip to get first pickings.

"Okay, *now*," I told Blindboy.

We began clawing the slime away from the surface to get to the thing he'd heard down below. The stench was terrible. The stink on top of the dump is bad enough, but down below it makes people gag like they're about to vomit. Me and Blindboy, we don't puke anymore because we're used to it, like all the dump kids who've been around for a while.

Blindboy, he's the finder. Me, I'm the fixer. Hotwire and Blindboy, that's us. A team.

Blindboy can hear things, electrical junk, down below the ground. Electronic gadgets are usually still live in some way even though they're broken. Their circuits have capacitors and other components, which have stored energy. Live circuits let out tones that humans can't hear, but bats, dogs and cats, and of course Blindboy, *they* can hear them.

We've got a metal rod we push into the soft earth of the dumps, boring down below the slime, below the swill and dregs, the ordinary trash, until we hit something solid. Sometimes it's just a bottle. You can feel the grating of metal on glass, maybe hear the squeaking noise. Sometimes it's a stone or a brick. But occasionally, when we're lucky, it's a junked toaster, kettle, or radio someone's chucked out as useless.

Blindboy puts his ear close to the ground and he can hear if it's a kitchen gadget, or a luxury thing like a radio, just by listening to the electronic buzz. What it is, is this: Blindboy can't see, but he can hear ultrasonic sounds.

Once we've found something worth anything, then it's my job to fix it up so it works. I've got a sort of natural talent for fixing electronic gadgets. I can knit a few wires together and get a radio blasting inside a few minutes. I can take three bust-up kitchen mixers and make one good one. I can overhaul a broken fridge and get it going so's we can sell it by the roadside.

My dad was an electronics expert. I learned everything from him. My dad once said to me, "You're a real hotwire. I never saw a girl so fast with her fingers. You've got a real natural skill there." That's how come I'm called Hotwire now.

While we were working away, someone found something on the other side of the dump. The stupid kid got so excited she let out a great yell, so everyone else, from the tyke in the sawed-off spacerjeans to big Buzzard, who had yelled at us, all went running in that direction. While they were gone, we dug up our find.

"Hey, Blindboy, we've got a freezer!" I breathed.

4

"Yeah?" He half turned his face toward me. "What's it like? Can you fix it? Can we get a good price?"

"Not a big one," I said. "You feel it. It's about half a meter square. Probably it's from one of those big yachts in the harbor. Looks good, though. No bad marks on it. Paint's good."

"But can you fix it?" repeated Blindboy.

"I can fix anything," I bragged.

I'm a bit like that. I show off sometimes. I can't help it. It's in my nature. Well, when you're a dump kid, you've got to have *something* to brag about, because otherwise you'd be a nothing, a yerk. There are thousands of people who have so much money they've got nothing left to buy. They don't need to brag because they *know* what they've got.

Then there are the rest of us, millions of people, eating cabbage stalks from the gutter because we're so poor. But that's life, isn't it? So far as I know, it's never been any different. When you're one of the cabbage-stalk eaters, you find something you can do that no one else can, and you show off with it. That's human nature.

"Let's drag it down near the road before the other kids come back," I said to Blindboy.

We heaved and pushed the freezer to the edge of the greasy slope and then slid it down the slime to the bottom. Blindboy sat on the fridge to protect it while I went and got a rag to wipe it down. We made it look real good. Then I went into the back of it and pulled out its guts. There were four cards of electronic components.

In the pockets of my overalls I always carry dozens of tiny transistors, resistors, capacitors, and other pieces. I've also got a small tool kit, built up from finds on the dump. My most swazz tool is a do-it-yourself welder, which works from batteries. In no time at all I had cut out the dud bits and hotwired good ones in their places. There was still something left in the freezer's power pack, and the whole appliance hummed like a happy robot.

"Hey!" cried Blindboy. "You made it work!"

"'Course I made it work, you nut," I said. "Help me drag it to the edge of the highway."

Once we got it there we chalked a sign that said FREEZER FOR SALE: GOING DIRT CHEAP.

We sat there for an hour while the zipcars whizzed past, their drivers not even looking. Then finally a skidder pulled up and a woman leaned out the side window.

"What you got there, kids?"

"*An elephant*," I muttered, but then I shouted, "Nice freezer, lady, in fine working order."

She looked the freezer up and down twice. "Looks okay, Frank," she said to someone in the car. "We could put it in the boathouse."

Frank said something I couldn't hear; then the skidder pulled out into the traffic again.

No deal. Frank didn't like our freezer. Right at that moment I wished Frank would get gangrene of the brain. Blindboy yelled, "Cheap yerkies!" after them. It didn't do any good, but it made us both feel better. We settled down again, hoping someone else would stop.

Finally, a fat man in a big skidder pulled over. He got out, looked at the freezer, and said, "You found this in the dump?"

"So what?" said Blindboy, obviously not liking the sound of the voice.

"So it's public property. I can just take it."

"I fixed it up to work," I said.

"Go home, little girl." The man laughed. "You couldn't fix yourself up with a good wash, let alone repair a freezer."

We'd had this kind of highway robbery before and I knew how to deal with it. I ran between the man and his skidder.

"You touch our freezer without paying for it," I warned, "and I'll bite you. I'll break the skin—you see if I don't."

The man paled a little, though he tried to look angry. "You'll *what*?"

"I'll bite your stupid leg. I've got all sorts of diseases

on my teeth, from eating slime on the dump. If you want to catch something nasty, just try taking that freezer."

"Her teeth are worse than a rat's," Blindboy confirmed. "People have got rabies from her bites." This wasn't exactly true—Blindboy always overdoes things. Still, the man was uncertain. He knew he could grab hold of me and hit me, but he couldn't avoid me and he couldn't be sure I wouldn't bite him while we struggled.

"Don't you *dare* bite me," he hissed.

"You'll be infected right away. I've got really bad teeth." I bared them for his inspection.

The man took out a wallet and threw a bill to the ground.

"All right," he growled, "that's for the freezer. Now let me go past. No biting, mind."

He gathered the freezer in his arms and walked toward me, cautiously. I ran around him and picked up the money. It wasn't a whole lot, but it would get us some Frizzo to drink. We watched him put the freezer in his family skidder. Then he went over to the driver's seat.

"This isn't much!" I said, waving the bill. "That's some freezer you've got there."

"It's all you're getting," grunted the fat man. Then he suddenly stared at Blindboy. "What's the matter with him?" he asked.

"He can't see," I replied. "He's blind."

"Can't he beg?" said the man.

"We aren't beggars," shouted Blindboy furiously. "We work for our living."

The man nodded, slowly, then climbed into his skidder. Before he slipped away into the traffic his hand came out of the window, another bill between his thumb and forefinger. He let it go after about two seconds and it floated to the ground. It was bigger than the one we already had. I grabbed it quick.

"Just enough!" I yelled ungratefully after the disappearing skidder.

I told Blindboy how much we'd got.

"That's better," he said, "only he should have given it to us whether I can see or not. The freezer was worth that much, wasn't it, Hotwire?"

"It sure was, Blindboy," I replied. "Now let's forget him. We can eat burgers tonight."

Blindboy's face broke into a smile. "Yeah," he said, grinning. "Burgers and Frizzo!"

We set off across the dump, for the city.

2

The city was crackling that night, as it always crackled. There were thousands of people on the streets; some of them never went anywhere else. They lived there. They built fires on the street corners to keep themselves warm. Others had homes to go to, but not always good homes. Just derelict ruins, not much more than shells. The rich people came in their skidders, wazzoos, benders, and other kinds of zipcars. They used parking lots under the stores, so you hardly saw them on the street.

There was a light drizzle in the air.

Just a couple of days before, Blindboy had found an old motherboard that I had now fixed. It was in good working order and was worth about five dollars to any computer junk artist. On its own it was no good to anyone, but with a lot of other parts it could be used to complete a handmade computer.

In the middle of the market district was a large slum building sectioned off into dozens of open-fronted shops. In each of these small shops there were piles of computer parts: junk hardware cannibalized from broken computers. One or two technicians sat in the front of each shop, building handmade computers from the junk.

The place where all this rewiring and soldering was carried out was called The Golden Arcade. Most of the technicians worked with a speed and confidence that amazed onlookers. You went in, chose your shop, stated your requirements, and a technician would whip it out for you out of junk parts in thirty minutes flat. Cheap too.

The Golden Arcade was the place to take any computer junk we found in the dump, only we were always cheated by the shop owners there. They knew that dump kids couldn't sell the stuff anywhere else, so they gave us next to nothing for it. We had to take what we could get.

Some kids tried to pirate illegal software in The Golden Arcade, but if you got caught the big companies got really vicious. They didn't have any soul and being a kid wouldn't save you. They would make sure you got banged in good, and it wasn't worth it. Generally me and Blindboy didn't do illegal stuff because sooner or later you got caught.

Blindboy and me went through the fish and vegetable market first, which was on the outer edge of the market district. There was everything for sale there—and in some cases almost nothing. One old lady I saw had a row of six spring onions she was hoping to sell. Those six onions, laid out neatly on a rag, were probably the only thing she owned in the world and stood between her and starvation. If she didn't manage to sell them she could always eat them, but onions are not very kind to an empty stomach. She'd do better with bread. I bought a stale two-cent bread roll from another stall and gave it to her. Blindboy and me had plenty anyway.

Next we had to wend our way through the zipcar junk stalls, the TV area, and the old-clothes section before we finally reached The Golden Arcade.

We went straight to Gipsie Hall, one of the shop owners who dealt with dump kids, and I took the board out of my pocket.

"How much?" I asked her.

"Fifty cents," she said, without even looking up.

"Fifty cents!" cried Blindboy. "It's worth at least five dollars. Give us two."

"Seventy-five cents. Last offer."

And she wouldn't budge from there.

We took it and left, heading for the neon lights.

"There's a burger stall," I said to Blindboy, who was clinging to the belt of my overalls. "Let's go get some real food."

All around us there were signs fizzing and sparking, lighting up the wet roadway with colors. It was hard not to be jostled while you were in the streets because not only were there too many people but the traders' goods spilled out of their shopfronts and onto the pavement. Even in the neon-light district, pots and pans, magazines, fruit and vegetables, baskets of chickens, and radio junk all blocked the way.

If you stepped out into the road, though, you stood a chance of being run down by a commuter's wazzoo. So we pushed our way through the forest of legs to the burger stall and bought two Bamwamburgers and a Frizzo each. While we were standing there eating and drinking, a woman pulled up to the curb in a nice new low-slung skidder. She must have been in a hurry, because she looked wealthy and rich people didn't often park on the street.

She got out and locked the skidder with a tonal key.

While the woman was in the store I noticed a tall, thin man with spiked hair, staring at the zipcar. He was chewing a Frizzo straw and looking thoughtful. I guessed what he was thinking. He was wondering if he could get into the skidder and take what he could lay his hands on before the woman came back. Either that or he was planning to steal the zipcar itself.

13

However, someone came along who made up his mind for him. A motozip cop on his city machine wheeled through the traffic and came up to the burger stall. He climbed off his zip and pulled off his gloves.

"Gimme a sandwich and a coffee, Charlie," said the cop. "Usual filling." Then his nose twitched and he looked down at us. "You kids smell," he said.

"So would you if you lived on the dump," snapped back Blindboy.

I nudged him. "It's a cop," I said.

Blindboy nodded. "I know it's a cop. I heard the motozip; then I heard him take off his gloves."

The cop removed his helmet.

"You kids give me any lip and I'll crack your shins, you hear me?"

"We hear you," I said, pulling Blindboy away before he got us into trouble.

At that moment the woman came out of the store and took out her tonal key. She pressed the button several times, but the car remained locked.

"Crit!" she cried. "It's not working."

"Let me try, lady," said the cop, coming to her rescue. I was glad to see the key didn't work for him either.

Blindboy stopped sucking his Frizzo and said quietly, "You're using the wrong key, lady."

"What?" she said.

"You used a different key when you locked your skidder."

The cop looked down at Blindboy. "How'd you know that, smarty?"

"The tones are different now," said Blindboy, "from what they were the first time."

The cop looked at him again and then waved his hand in contempt.

Meanwhile, the woman stood staring at her key. "Wait a minute," she said, "the boy's right. This is the key to my husband's bender." She searched through her bag and came out with another key. When she tried pressing it I heard the door to her skidder unlocking. She seemed relieved.

"Thank goodness. Can I give you something, little boy?" she said, rooting through her bag.

"That's not necessary," said the cop.

"If the lady wants to give us something what's it to you?" I said to the cop.

The cop glared at me. "I told you to watch your lip."

By this time the woman had slipped something into Blindboy's hand. We moved on without a second glance at the policeman. "How much did you get?" I asked Blindboy.

"Feels like a ten." He grinned.

I yelled, "Hey, this is our lucky day—but we'd

better spend it before we go back to the dump. You can't hide money from the other kids—they'd smell it a mile off. Unless . . ."

" 'Less what?"

"Unless we buy something and take it back to share. But it's your money, Blindboy, so you get to say."

He stared at me in that sightless way of his.

"It's *our* money, Hotwire. Let's go and get some rice chips and more Frizzo. . . ."

We turned against the current of people, which was flowing like a flood tide along the street, and crossed over. When we reached the other curb I felt a hand on my shoulder and whirled around to face the thin man who had been staring at the skidder outside the store.

"Hi, kids," he said, his smile a bit like a slash in a watermelon. Although he was tall, he seemed bent in the middle, so that he leaned over us. "That was a pretty swazz trick you pulled over there." His voice was high and excited, with a twang to some of the words, as if some hidden guitar player was helping him speak by flicking his vocal cords. He jerked his head in the direction of the burger stall. "You got the farsighted gift, eh?"

"Do what?" I asked.

"The other kid. He saw which key she used the first time, yeah?"

The man's eyes were like pinpoints of light set in a dark void.

"You kerk," said Blindboy. "I've got no eyes."

"Yeah," laughed the man. "But if you didn't *see* it was a different key, how did you *know* the tones was different? I mean, you can't hear nothin' when someone uses one of them keys. I think you're fakin' something. You got some kind of scam going to cheat tips out of ladies."

I was a little wary of this strange kerk and began to say Blindboy was just lucky, but Blindboy broke in hotly with, "Listen mister, if I say I can hear the tones, I can *hear* 'em. You calling me a liar?"

The man's eyes widened and so did his red, wet grin. I thought his head was going to split in two. He rubbed his thin hands together quickly with a rasping sound, like his flesh was made of some kind of sandpaper. The rapid movements made the thongs on his simleather jacket lash like whips at his forearms with a swishing noise. *Rasp, swish, rasp, swish.* He was a real street snake.

"You can really hear those things? Those tones?"

"So what?" said Blindboy, still angry.

"So what? So *what?*" cried the man. "So you could listen to a key, hear the tones, and make another key just like it, right?"

Blindboy began to catch some of my caution, now that his anger was going. He said, "Maybe."

17

"Look," said the man, very excited now, "they call me Kevin A. What d'they call you kids?"

"Hotwire and Blindboy," I said.

"Don't you have any real names?"

"Don't need 'em," I snapped. "We like what we call ourselves. Any objections?"

"None at all. Where you hang out? You're dump kids, right?"

I didn't reply to this.

He nodded gravely.

"Pretty rough life. I was a dump kid at your age. Now look at me. Good clothes, plenty to eat—"

I interrupted with, "How come you're so skinny then?"

He laughed at this. It sounded like a sewer unclogging. "I've got a nervous disposition, that's why. I burn it off. Believe me, I have plenty of money. Anyways, I'll see you kids around, okay? Maybe I'll come visit the dump tomorrow. How's that? You be there?"

"Maybe." I shrugged. "Maybe not. We're not *always* there," I said. I wasn't sure we wanted to see him again.

o——o

When we got back to the dump we shared the food with the kids in our section. We sat on the plateau of rubbish and stared over at the sparkling city. The streets looked as if they were encrusted with jewels: a rich kingdom of the night. One day me and Blindboy were going to live in the city, when we had a really good find and made a lot of money. That's if one of us didn't get sick and die, like some kids do. It was all dependent on finding a good piece of junk.

There's a difference between types of rubbish, by the way; at least there is to us dump kids. Trash is stuff that's completely useless to anyone, like, say, a squashed plastic container with a hole in it. Garbage is stuff like newspapers, bits of string, cardboard boxes: partly useful stuff but not valuable. Slime is swill, sloppy foodstuffs, which we eat when there's no money around. Junk is broken kitchen appliances and gadgets: very useful, obviously.

You can't afford to let yourself get too down about being on the dump, because that's all us kids have got. But sometimes I get this sort of choky feeling, as if I just want to get up and run—run till I drop—to get away from the stink and dirt, find someplace where there's some clean air to breathe. It comes over me like a panic and I have to start talking fast to somebody, even *myself* if I'm on my own, until the feeling goes away and I can get jokey about it all again.

"There's the ghost of a robot vacuum cleaner, over on the other side of the dump," said a kid called Oilslick, making us stare out into the blackness around us. "When you're asleep it comes and sucks the breath out of you. . . ."

I glanced up at the stars for comfort. "You stop that scary talk," I said. "I don't like it."

"That's 'cause you're a *girl*," sneered Oilslick.

This made me rocket mad—it had nothing to do with anything. Oilslick always said stupid things like that when he was looking for attention. I bunched my fists.

"You wanna say that again?"

Oilslick ignored me, smiled, and carried on with the story.

"I can smell 'em tonight, the evil machines on their midnight walk. They're coming to get us and rob our souls from our bodies. Feel that sort of tickle on your ear? That's the ghost of a gadget, trying to suck your spirit through your ear hole."

Half a dozen kids squealed and slapped their hands over their ears.

"Listen!" said Oilslick. "You can hear 'em moving deep under the trash! Just a click here, a squeak there. Sometimes they swim through the sludge to the top and burst through, their mechanical parts dripping with stinkin' gore, their red lights glowing like terrible eyes, roamin' around in the dark looking for kids to make into zombie slaves, to drag them down into the world below the dump, where they suffocate forever on slime."

All the kids went quiet, their eyes wide open, listening for the evil machines, until I couldn't stand it any longer.

"I'm going to bed," I shouted, leaping to my feet and making just about everyone jump with fright.

Blindboy said, "Aw, you mess up all the fun, Hotwire. I *like* it when Oilslick talks like that. Gives me a really wavy feeling in my stomach."

"How come you like it?" I cried, confused. "I can't sleep if I think something's coming to get me. How can you sleep? I hate it. My head's full of stuff now."

Blindboy shrugged. "I just like it."

So I went off to bed and crawled underneath my polyethylene tent. It was held up in the middle with a wazzoo axle and around the edges there were bricks. It kept out the wind and wet and made a slide for the rats. I had a piece of old carpet to lie on and a tire for a pillow.

After an hour it began to rain and the other kids all came to bed too. Blindboy, in the tent next to mine, fell asleep straight off—I could see him through his polyethylene—while I still lay awake, scared to close my eyes. I kept telling myself it was the noise of the rain on the plastic that kept me awake.

When the rain stopped and the moon came out, I

had no excuse. So I tried to concentrate on the rats that ran up and skidded down the polyethylene, staring at their underbellies, their small claws, their bright little eyes, their tiny red mouths full of white needles.

In the middle of the night I suddenly woke up to the sound of screaming. Outside the moon had disappeared behind some cloud and it was pitch-black. I guessed it was about two-thirty. The screaming was high-pitched, full of terror; my heart started racing with fear. It went on for a few more minutes and then it suddenly stopped.

Just as I was trying to get to sleep again, there was a scrabbling at the polyethylene.

I sat up quickly, all my nerves on edge. I felt down beside the edge of the polyethylene, where I kept a piece of iron bar. I gripped it, hoping it wasn't necessary.

"Who's that?" I whispered, my voice sounding hoarse.

There was a sobbing sound, then, "It's me. Muffler."

The stiffness went out of my body as my muscles relaxed. I let go of the iron bar. Muffler was one of the kids who lived on the north side of the dump. She shared a tent with Sofa, a little fat girl.

"What is it?" I asked quietly, not wanting to wake up Blindboy.

"They come and took away Sofa."

I let this sink in before lifting the flap and staring into the dark face of Muffler. All I could see was a glint in her eyes, where the tears glistened.

"Who took her?" I asked.

Muffler sniffled. "I dunno. Some men. They just come in and dragged her off. They just took her away."

A chill went through me. Things like this happened to kids on the dump. There was no one here to look after us. In the day we tried to band together, help each other, protect each other, but it wasn't easy at night. In any case, if someone really wanted to get you, they would.

"Why'd they take her?" I said, knowing it was a useless question. There could be any number of reasons, some of which were too horrible to think about. Sometimes bodies turned up back here in the dump, under the slime. There were some evil people in the world and we were prey to the worst of them.

"Maybe 'cause she's a girl?" said Muffler, still crying. "I just run off when they come. I couldn't help it. They would've took me too." But the fact that Sofa was a girl was no reason. They took boys too. Especially the small ones.

"You want to come in here for a while?" I said to Muffler.

"Yes, please, Hotwire."

She crawled in beside me and we cuddled up. Muffler lay shivering for a long time. As soon as the sky showed some light, she left the tent. I guess she wanted to look for Sofa, to see if she could find any trace of her. I didn't hold out much hope. I tried to imagine what I would do if someone came and took away Blindboy; I gritted my teeth, thinking how I would smash them to bits with my iron bar. It was all just thoughts really, because when it came down to it we weren't strong enough to watch out for each other. We were just kids.

Finally I dropped off, into a deep sleep.

3

I woke up with a hot autumn sun shining through the polyethylene. It was difficult to see out through the misted sheeting; my clothes were steaming and filling the tent with vapor. I got up and went out, looking for a bowl of water.

When dump kids find plastic bowls or buckets without holes in them, they lay them out to catch the rainwater. I found a full container and had a drink. My dad taught me hygiene before he died, and one of the things he insisted on was a morning wash, so I gave myself a lick and a promise.

Next I roused Blindboy, who always sleeps in past everyone else. He grumbled, but he finally came out of his cozy tent and I gave him some water to wash with. Then we went looking for crusts of bread for breakfast. Once that was done we went to work with the rod, looking for junk under the slime. Mostly we worked around the section where the rubbish wazzoo-trucks were pumping out their new loads.

Like the seagulls we flocked to the most recent rub-bish. There was little difference between us and the bird scavengers except that somehow they managed to stay clean. There were wild dogs and feral cats there too. We battled each other for the tidbits that came off the back of the wazzootrucks, though of course the men who drove them had taken first pick of everything before we even saw it.

Halfway through the morning, while I was trying to fix a shaver Blindboy had uncovered, a man came striding through the kids. "Where's Blindboy and Hotwire?" he called.

It was Kevin A, the spiky-haired street snake.

I knew why he was having trouble finding us: when dump kids have been in the slime for a few hours they're impossible to tell apart. All he could see was a hundred or so dirty faces with eyes in them. There was a lot of confusion too, with dogs running between legs, chasing cats, and cats trying to jump on seagulls before they took off.

A big kid called Fridge said, "Who wants to know?"

I tried to duck out of sight, but then Kevin A turned in our direction, peered as though looking into a dark room, and strode over to us. He found it hard to walk on the dump in his high-heeled boots. If he had ever really been a dump kid, he would've known that wearing boots like his was stupid here.

My guess was Kevin A was an outzoner who'd come to the city on the make and had been taken in by street snakes to do their errands for them. He dressed too cheap and glitzy for an ex–dump kid. He didn't seem to have any idea of quality clothes. You get to know about things like that on the dump. Expensive rags and leathers end up here, not just cheap, shoddy goods, and a dump kid gets to know the difference between quiet stylish shoes and tasteless flashy boots.

"Hi, kids," he croaked. He took out a pack of sweetsticks. "You want one?" he asked.

"Naw," I said. "Me and Blindboy don't smoke them things."

Kevin A shrugged and lit one for himself, sucking in deeply until the colored smoke came through his nostrils. I only tried to smoke sweetsticks once; for three days afterward it felt like someone was driving a wazzootruck around inside my head. The pain just wasn't worth it.

"What you got there?" he asked.

"A shaver, but there's too many parts missing," I said, throwing the item away.

Kevin A folded in the middle as he bent down to talk to us, holding the sweetstick vertically as if it were a little flag. His breath smelled like a nightclub bouncer's armpit. I felt like gagging, but some grease had run from his slicked-back hair and trickled down the left side of his nose, fascinating me. I stood sniffing his after-breath, wrinkling my nose, and watching the gobbet of grease roll down through the angular valley between his cheekbone and his nostril.

"Listen, kids," said Kevin A in a businesslike voice, "I got some work for you. I wanna give this to you on account." He took out two tens and offered us one each. We took them of course, then waited for the catch. "Just a little bit of work is all," said Kevin A.

"What work?" said Blindboy, turning his eyes in the direction of the voice.

"Yeah, easy work—for you two. A friend of mine, he's, well, he's got a problem. We think you can help us out with it. It's sort of fixing an electronic gadget. How about it? You get paid."

"How much?" I asked.

"Girl," he said, "you get fifty. The blind boy gets thirty."

"We both get sixty," I said.

Kevin A flicked his sweetstick away with an annoyed expression. "Hey!" he said.

Blindboy rapped, "Sixty each or nothing, slummer."

Kevin A stared at us with the same annoyed expression on his face, then suddenly smiled his watermelon-slit smile. His twangy voice rose, his expression changing to one of forced pleasantness. "Sixty? That's fine. You do a good job for me and you each get your sixty, how's that?"

We nodded and followed Kevin A across the plateau of rubbish. He was slow because of his high heels and he kept cursing when he sank in the mire. There was also a constant stream of complaints from his lips about the stench.

"You said you used to live here," I told him. "Didn't you get used to it like us kids?"

"When you've been away from it for as long as I have, you never want to get used to it again," he said.

Finally we made the city streets and Kevin A took us directly to a public bathhouse. He paid for a bath and we went in one at a time to scrub ourselves clean.

"We got to get rid of those rags too," he said when we came out. "They stink." He took us to a second-hand shop and we rooted through clothes similar to those we found on the dump, only this stuff had been washed. I picked out a pair of jeans and a sweatshirt with CEREBRAL CHROME written over the front. I didn't know what it meant, but it sounded swazz. I chose Blindboy some sailor's pants and a striped sweater. The pants were too long of course, but we cut off the bottoms with a pair of scissors the clerk let us borrow.

"Are they yellow?" asked Blindboy. "I hate yellow."

"They're blue," I said. "Both of them."

"Good, because I hate yellow."

Kevin A, who was told during our walk to the shop that Blindboy had been sightless since birth, gave Blindboy a funny look. "How does he know what yellow looks like?" he asked me. He treated Blindboy as if he were deaf as well as blind, which made Blindboy mad.

Blindboy snapped, "I've got colors in my head, you kerk."

Kevin A was already learning to ignore the insults in Blindboy's outbursts. "Yeah," he said, "but how does he know which color is which?"

"Well, yellow's not red, blue, green, or any other color, is it?" said Blindboy.

Kevin A shook his head slowly. "No, it ain't."

"Then," said Blindboy as if the man were stupid, "it must be yellow, mustn't it?"

I could see by Kevin A's face that he was having trouble working this out, but he didn't say any more about it. Instead he ushered us out of the shop and led us along the street to a nice shiny bender. Then Kevin A drove us to a tall building in the heart of the city. Once we were inside we took an elevator to the seventh floor.

In the elevator Kevin A said, "I don't see what it matters which color you wear. You can't see it anyway, can you?"

"Other people can," growled Blindboy. "I don't want people to think I'm a banana, do I?"

We went past several burly-looking men in sharp clothes whose faces looked like they'd been hammered flat with a wooden stake. They looked as if they didn't have a smile to share among them. Kevin A then pushed me and Blindboy gently into an office. Sitting behind a large desk was a small man with wizened features. He nodded at Kevin A.

"These the kids you spoke about?" asked the man in a soft, fatherly voice. I know how a father talks, because I've had one, and sometimes they use this sort of gentle dimsum tone when they want you to feel good.

"Yes, sir," said Kevin A respectfully.

The man then smiled at us, his tanned face crumpling into a thrown-away paper bag. His eyes were really weird—bright—like they had small lit-up bulbs behind them. When he picked up his pen you could see his stubby fingers were strong, though, and probably joined to strong arms. He looked like he could strangle a dump dog with one hand, and I bet he would do it too. I bet he would strangle *anyone* without thinking too hard about whether it was the right thing to do.

Kevin A left us alone with the man in the office.

We were told to sit down on a couch, and the little man studied us with those small lightbulb eyes. I felt a bit nervous and out of my depth, which was why I wasn't saying much. The whole thing was bewildering for both me and Blindboy. We weren't used to being treated like human beings, and I was overawed in any case. I could tell Blindboy was none too comfortable either. He couldn't see our surroundings of course, the fancy office with its thick carpets and swazz furniture, but he could smell and touch everything. The couch we were sitting on was soft leather and the scent of flowers was coming from somewhere.

"Listen to this," said the little man behind the desk, and he pressed a button on a recorder.

After a while I said, "I can't hear nothing."

The man stood up. He was just a bit taller than me, but he moved like a weight lifter, as if his muscles were getting in each other's way. He walked over to Blindboy and stared down at him as if he could see inside Blindboy's head.

"No, but *he* can, can't you, blind kid?"

Blindboy nodded. "Some tones," he said. "Key tones."

"Right!" cried the man. "Now you, girl. See that device on the table next to you?"

I looked down and saw an instrument with piano keys.

"I see it."

"I want you to start pressing those keys. You, the blind one, when you hear a tone identical to the first one you heard on this recorder, tell the girl to stop."

I began pressing down the keys, one by one, not hearing anything myself of course. Blindboy was listening intently beside me. When I came to the fourth key, Blindboy told me to stop. We then went on through the scale and back again until we had the tones that had been on the recorder, all in their right order.

The little man seemed very pleased. "Terrific. Fine. We can make a key now that we know what the tones are."

"Make a key?" I said. Copying tonal keys was illegal.

The little man looked at me sharply, then smiled, his face creasing like crumpled paper. "Yes. It's all right—don't look so worried. Everything is aboveboard. You have my guarantee on that." His voice was very soothing and reassuring.

I was worried, though. Me and Blindboy normally steered clear of things like this. Then again, sixty each was a lot of money. It would keep us for a long time if we could find somewhere safe to hide it and take it out bill by bill. Maybe just this once wouldn't hurt, especially when everything looked very respectable anyway with the office and carpet and all.

The man behind the desk said, "I hear you're pretty good with electronics, girl. How about making us the new key. Everything's fine, so you just go ahead."

Kevin A came back in the office, looking like a tent pole next to the squat old man. He led us into a side room, where there was a tonal key and some tools. Now that I knew what frequencies to set for the tones, it didn't take me more than a few minutes to program the key. The little man was delighted when we gave it to him. "Good, good," he said. "Now, Kevin A said we settled on sixty each as a price for the work. Is that right?"

Blindboy said, "That's right."

He opened a wallet and passed us ten each. "That's on account. I don't want you to spend a hundred and twenty all at once. It would look suspicious. When you get through the tens, go to Kevin A and he'll give you some more. But not all in one day. There must be at least two clear days before you each get another ten, you understand me?"

Somehow the tone of his voice did not encourage us to argue with him. We took the tens in silence and Kevin A led us from the office. Just before we went through the door, the man behind the desk called out, "Don't forget, you work for Mouseman now. Just keep your mouths shut and you'll be looked after. See that they get looked after, Kevin A."

"Yes, sir," said Kevin A, pushing us out into the corridor with a lazy shove of his hand.

We tramped past the bulky men whose job seemed

to be to wander backward and forward along the corridors without smiling. My thoughts were in a turmoil. He had said we worked for Mouseman. The neon news screens in the city square were always displaying that name. Mouseman was a big crime boss who ran the south side of the city. The police had been trying to catch him for years, without success. Somehow he always managed to escape the law.

Blindboy said in the elevator, "That man's a crook, Hotwire."

"I know," I said, looking at Kevin A. "And what's more, he owes us money. You brought us here, man; you pay us the rest of our money. We want to go back to the dump now."

Kevin A shrugged. "You work for us now."

"We don't work for crooks," snapped Blindboy.

Kevin A's pinpointy eyes had a cruel look deep inside their tiny pupils.

"You got no choice," he said. "You just broke the law by making a tonal key. That's illegal. I could turn you over to the cops now if I wanted."

"You asked us to make it," shouted Blindboy. "You'd go down too when we told them."

Kevin A bent over Blindboy like some giant predatory bird, as if he were going to eat him whole.

"You don't get it, do you, kid? We stuff the key in your pocket, see, and we drop you out of a skidder at some traffic cop's feet. If you try to get us involved, then the cops won't have you for long. We'll get you out and give you a final bath in the canal—facedown."

Kevin A let this sink in before adding, "Of course, even if you don't talk you'll end up in the kids' sweatrooms."

Fear dribbled like ice water into my brain. Every dump kid dreaded the sweatrooms. They used you like slaves, locking you in windowless rooms to work sixteen hours a day on circuit boards for computers. There was a window, with a view to show you what you were missing outside—but it was *painted* on the wall. The air was stale and stifling and dried the snot in your nose to concrete, dried your eyes until they felt like they were full of grit.

One component was all you ever got to fit to the board. One little transistor or wire, day in, day out. It was more than boring, it was mind-crushing. By the time you were sixteen, you were a glass-eyed zombie with a brain like mushy peas. It was ten times worse than the dump.

What was more, once they had you inside, you weren't likely to come out again—not until you were old enough to go to prison. Then they threw you out into the city streets again, just when you'd become totally dependent on the institution.

Blindboy's fingers slipped into my hand. "I don't want to go to the sweatrooms," he whispered.

Neither did I. It looked like we were working for Mouseman, until we could get out of it somehow. Maybe we could run away, to some other city? Take a rail rattler out of this part of the country? But we didn't know any other cities. For the time being we were stuck.

4

That night, back at the dump, I didn't even bother to go to the storytelling. I just lay in my tent staring up at the stars, wondering what was going to become of Blindboy and me. To a certain extent I was to blame. I knew, even while we were doing it, that messing around with key tones was illegal. I should have said, "Hey, what are we doing here, Blindboy? Let's leave—now."

Instead I had pushed any doubts aside with the vague thought that a good explanation would be given at the end of it all. An explanation that would put our minds at rest.

Now we were mixed up with Mouseman, one of the most dangerous criminals in the city. I didn't know what to do about it. If I went to the police and told them what had happened they might throw me and

Blindboy in the sweatrooms. Besides, making a key was not a serious offense to a man like Mouseman. His lawyers would have him out of jail within the hour, while we might end up stuck in the sweatrooms forever.

I heard a whisper at the entrance to my tent. "Hotwire?" It was Blindboy. He came inside and lay down next to me. "We're in trouble, aren't we?" he said.

"Yes, but what we've got to do is face it out. Maybe they'll forget about us and just leave us here. If we have to do something else for them, we'll do it wrong, or make excuses that it's too hard for us, something like that."

"Will they believe us?"

"I don't know," I said, sensing deep inside that they never would.

○──○

After a restless night's sleep we went down to the city square, and there, above the bustling market stalls, emblazoned in neon, was the latest news:

○ COMPUTER CODES BURGLARY ○

Last night the offices of Complex Computer Company were burgled. Several volumes of binary codes were taken from the scene of the crime. These are believed to be the access codes associated with the computer network of clearing banks. The police have asked for any information from the public as to the possible whereabouts of the codes or who might be responsible for the theft.

I felt as if I had a huge fat man standing on my chest. I hadn't any doubt who was responsible for the crime or how they had got into the offices. I was certain that I had made the key to the vault that had contained the computer codes and Blindboy had supplied me with the tones for that key. People flowed around us, occasionally jostling us as we stood there like a pair of statues, but I hardly noticed them.

"What is it?" asked Blindboy, sensing that something was bothering me.

"Somebody's pinched some computer books," I said.

"What books?"

"Codes to the banks."

Blindboy sucked in his breath noisily. "That means they'll be able to access people's accounts from a hidden terminal and steal their money, doesn't it?"

I didn't have to answer, any more than I had to explain to Blindboy that we were mixed up in this thing as deeply as any crook. Blindboy couldn't see, but he knew what was going on just as well as I did.

Blindboy said after a while, "This is pretty big stuff,

Hotwire. I don't want any more of Mouseman's money—"

Just then he was interrupted by the clamping of a hand on each of our necks. I jumped at least a klick high before turning. I expected to see a policeman behind me, but it was watermelon face. Almost as bad.

"Kevin A," I said cheerfully, before Blindboy could blurt out something we both might regret. "How are you?"

"I'm fine, kids," said Kevin A, releasing us. "More to the point, how are *you*? You over the shock yet, being members of the underworld?"

He gave us one of his famous thin grins.

"Oh, sure." I smiled back, trying to look nonchalant. "What the smiff do we care about cops, eh? I mean, what have people done for us? Two orphans, left to rake through the slime of a rubbish dump. Nothin', that's what. You have to take in this world, 'cause nobody's going to give a thing to you."

Kevin A slapped me on the back. "That's just how I felt, girl, when the Mouseman took *me* off the dump. He's a savior, that man."

"Alleluia!" said Blindboy, but Kevin A must have missed the sarcasm in the tone, because he just laughed and added, "Amen to that."

"So," I said, "we work for Mouseman now?"

Kevin A looked down at me and shook his head slowly. "Nooooo, girl. You work for *me*—and don't you forget it. I loaned you to Mouseman for a single job, but actually we're going to do things together, just the three of us. Mouseman don't mind if we earn a living. 'Course if he *requests* your help again you got to give it, but until that time the three of us gets our own work, see?"

"Listen," I said quickly, "we got to get back to the dump for a minute. . . ."

"No," said Kevin A. "You don't go back to no dump, ever. Last night was your last night, so to speak. Now you stay with me at the old warehouse, get it?"

"But we've got to say good-bye to . . ."

"To nobody, that's who." Kevin A smiled. "Forget it, girl. You and Blindboy, you're my little helpers now."

Kevin A took out a slim-bladed knife and began tapping with it in a manner that was full of meaning. Until now I had taken him for a bit of a clown, but I could see he was dangerous too. There was some of the street cobra in Kevin A. I had the feeling he could strike you dead with one sharp flash of blade and then walk away whistling.

I almost took to my heels and ran, then and there. But I couldn't do it. I couldn't abandon Blindboy to this alligator. For the time being, we had to go along with him and do as we were told.

Kevin A forced a passage through the people milling around the square, dragging Blindboy by the wrist. I followed on behind, hoping we would come across a policeman. It would be better to go to the sweatrooms, I was sure now, than to be slaves of Kevin A. However, as usual, just when you want a cop the streets are empty of them.

The snake took us to an old warehouse on an abandoned wharf. It had a thousand stairs leading to the higher rooms and no elevator to take us there. My legs were aching when we got to the top.

There he locked us in a room furnished with dirty rugs and boxes and a few luxury goods like a TV and a cocktail mixer. In one corner of the room was a pile of empty bottles. In another corner were three or four scruffy-looking futon mattresses. There were no windows and the high ceiling was a network of steel rafters that disappeared into a kind of black universe.

"Home Sweet Home," said our host.

Kevin A promised to return later with some food and drink, but in the meantime we were supposed to amuse ourselves. After searching for a way out and finding escape impossible, I switched on the TV. Some quiz show was on, with screeching people winning new zipcars. Blindboy sat by my side and listened without apparent interest. We both knew there was nothing we could do for the moment.

Kevin A returned later with some supplies. "You kids okay?" he asked.

"We're real swazz," said Blindboy sarcastically. "How are you, sir?"

Kevin A looked at him with narrow eyes. "You two eat," he said. "Then we're going out."

I had a peculiar sensation in my stomach. "Where are we going?" I asked.

"Wait and see" was the reply.

We ate the cold burgers and Frizzo he had brought us, trying to string out the time, but at ten-thirty Kevin A got to his feet.

"Okay, girl, and you, Blindboy, let's go. We got some work to do."

Reluctantly I got to my feet. Kevin A suddenly produced a pair of handcuffs and put one of the bracelets around Blindboy's wrist. The other he clipped around his own.

"Just to be sure you stay faithful to your Kevin A," he said, smirking. "We don't want you running away, do we? I hate sticking people in the back. I like to see their eyes when the blade goes in."

When we had climbed down the thousand stairs to the street, we found a bender parked by the curb. It was the same one Kevin A had used to take us to see Mouseman. We drove to a residential part of the city, where some of the rich people lived. There Kevin A parked the bender in the shadow of a tree.

We let two or three zipcars come and go from the houses. Eventually some wrought-iron gates opened down the street and a beautiful new sportsbender emerged. The gates closed behind it with a click and it roared off down the street. This was the sort of zipcar Kevin A had been waiting for and we followed it to the heart of the city. It went into a subterranean parking lot and we stayed on its tail.

The skidders, benders, and wazzoos were parked in stacks of ten. We pulled in three bays down from the sportsbender, but within earshot. Kevin A opened a window and said to Blindboy, "Listen!"

The owner of the sportsbender locked his vehicle and went toward the elevator. Kevin A, with Blindboy still manacled to his wrist, got out of our bender and went around to the trunk. From there Kevin A removed the piano device we had seen the day before. He played the keys, silently for me but not for Blindboy. Blindboy found the tones and I made the necessary adjustments to a spare key Kevin A had given me.

"Go and see if it works," Kevin A said, turning to me.

"What?"

"Go see if it works. If it does, get in and follow me back to the warehouse."

"Me?" I said wildly. "I can't drive."

"You better learn quick then," snapped Kevin A, "or I'll be cutting somebody soon."

"Don't worry about me, Hotwire," said Blindboy. "I couldn't give a smiff about him and his knife."

Kevin A jerked the chain to the handcuffs. "You better worry about it, girl, if you don't want no-eyes here to end up in the harbor."

Kevin A's face had a nasty look to it and I knew he meant it. It was obvious why he wanted *me* to drive the sportsbender. If we were caught going out of the lot, he could simply vanish.

I walked up to the sportsbender, held my breath, and pressed the key. There was a sullen clunking from the driver's door as the locks opened. I turned the door handle slowly and carefully. The fact was, I didn't want to disturb the alarm, which now had to be deactivated.

With the door wide open I felt carefully in all the obvious places: under the front rug, beneath the dashboard, in the door pocket, in the glove compartment, behind the rearview mirror. The owner of the car would know exactly where to look, of course, but I had to find wherever he had hidden the switch within a minute or the alarm would automatically trigger.

Then I saw them: two interior light switches. One of them had to be the alarm. I had a fifty-fifty chance. I chose the one on the left and winced as I switched it, expecting the alarm to suddenly pierce the hollow of the garage with its shrill note. Nothing happened. I had chosen the right switch.

Then I climbed into the passenger's seat and looked for the hood release. That was easy. Once the hood flipped up, I jumped out and went to work hotwiring the engine. It started purring immediately. Then I jumped back into the driver's seat.

It wasn't true that I did not know how to drive. I used to drive my dad's wazzoovan. But I'd never driven anything powerful like a sportsbender.

When I put my foot down the bender shot forward with a whoosh of air.

My head jerked back with the force. Concrete went past me like a river flowing in the other direction. I went stiff in every joint, expecting to collide with a pillar or wall at any moment. In my mind's eye I could see myself as a burger covered with ketchup— only it wouldn't be ketchup, it would just be the same color.

There was a whistling sound too. It took me a whole minute to realize the whistling was my own breath.

It was the sound of terror.

5

he bender missed the ten zipcars stacked in the bay by a fraction of a centimeter. My heart skidded over my ribs. I turned the vehicle in an arc, heading toward the exit, but I still didn't have full control over it. The sportsbender was too powerful for me: Just a light touch on the accelerator was enough to cause ripples on my cheeks from the G-force.

Fortunately, it was a new model, which meant the curbs along the exitway had a certain amount of control over the machine. When it headed alarmingly toward the walls, the magnetic force of the curbs pushed it back on course again. The street curbs would do the same once I got it outside. Still it was a rough ride, the bender snaking like mad as it zigzagged from one curb to the other.

I think I was supposed to stop at the barrier and

allow it to lift. I was so terrified, though, that I froze to the controls, jamming them. Instead of stopping and inserting the owner's card into the slot, I went crashing through, sending slivers of plastic scattering over the parking-garage floor. There was a *whap!* sound as the remainder of the barrier swung back as if batting an invisible ball.

Then I was out, zinging along the city streets.

I weaved between zipcars, sometimes so close to them that I could see the other drivers, their eyes large and round as I careened their way. It was a hair-raising ride but gradually I became used to the controls. By the time I stopped I had mastered the art of driving fairly straight.

I parked under a bridge and eventually Kevin A and Blindboy caught up with me. Kevin A leaped from his bender and came running up to the side window of my vehicle. "What in . . . ? Somebody put your brain in backward or what?" he yelled. He was so angry his nostrils were flaring red.

I was mad too. "I told you I can't drive," I yelled back.

Kevin A glared for another second, then walked around to the front of the sportsbender. He shook his head. "You've dented it now," he said. "When you hacked through that barrier, you dented the front."

He stamped back to his own vehicle and made a call on his pocket phone. Within a few minutes a skidder arrived and two men got out. They spoke briefly with Kevin A, then ordered me out of the driver's seat. One of the men climbed in and drove the vehicle away, toward the harbor. No doubt they were going to change its markings and paintwork so they could sell it at an auction.

"Get back into my bender," growled Kevin A.

I trudged over to Kevin A's vehicle and found Blindboy cuffed to one of the rear door handles. "You okay, Blindboy?" I asked.

His face had lit up a little on hearing my steps approaching. "I'm fine. What about you?"

"I'm still in one piece," I said, "but only because the god of dump girls was looking over me. It's a miracle I walked away from that sportsbender. It's vicious. It wanted to kill me."

Kevin A, right behind me after saying good-bye to his fellow thugs, said, "You drive like that again and *I'll* kill you."

"She *told* you she can't drive. It's your fault," said Blindboy.

Kevin A ordered us into the vehicle, then drove back to the warehouse in silence. Once again we were taken to his room and locked inside. We were given some cold pizza and water—not much better than what we'd be able to scrounge at the dump.

The pattern for our future as criminals was set.

We went out almost every day or night after that.

Kevin A would tell us what he wanted done and we would carry out his orders. Once we got used to stealing cars, it became a way of life. I'm not saying my conscience didn't bother me at all, because it did. Sometimes I woke up at night in a sweat, worrying about Blindboy—and about myself. We were now thieves, plain and simple, and we knew it was wrong. I felt bad after every robbery, but there was nothing we could do about it. If we wanted to live, we had to keep stealing for Kevin A.

When we weren't working, Kevin A locked us in the warehouse. We watched TV and stuff but still got bored, so I started carving things, animal figures mostly, out of hunks of wood I found lying around. I got so good at it I decided that if we ever got away, I'd try to sell some of these carvings.

Kevin A laughed when he saw one of them. "What's this supposed to be?" he asked.

"A dog. It's not *supposed* to be—it *is* a dog. Anyone can see that," I said, hurt by his jeering.

"Looks more like a *rat*," he said with a sneer. "Give it some whiskers and it'd be a dead ringer for a rat."

Blindboy said loyally, "I felt it. It feels like a dog."

"Well, it *looks* like a rat," repeated Kevin A.

One night, Kevin A made Blindboy hide in a corridor in a swazz apartment building and listen for a set of key tones. As usual, once he told me what they were, I made up a key. Once the key was made we went back to the same apartment. But this time Kevin A pushed us both toward the door. Me and Blindboy had to go in and pocket anything that would bring quick money.

It was Blindboy's job to stand at the door and listen for any approaching footsteps. "Give a whistle if anyone comes," I told him. I used the key to open the front door.

The apartment was lavishly furnished with soft rugs, chairs so deep you could fall into them, and highly polished tables. There were paintings on the walls, most of which I didn't like. There was a thick silk cover on the bed. I was tempted to take this, but it would have been too bulky. Instead I went to the dressing table and found some fancy boxes containing jewelry. I stuffed necklaces and bracelets into my pockets.

Next I searched the drawers for money but didn't find any. Most rich people used credit cards or computer terminals and didn't need to carry macrobucks. If a thief wanted cash it was best to rob a poor family, which I would never do, even if Kevin A tried to force me to. Only poor people had paper money, if they had any at all.

While I was looking around the bedroom I saw a

pic on a bedside table. It was in a really swazz silver frame with engraved flowers around the edge. There were two children, a boy and a girl about Blindboy's age, with their parents. They were all sitting on a sofa. The girl was looking up at her daddy and laughing as if he had just told a joke, while the boy was smiling into the camera. They all looked happy.

It gave me a funny feeling in my stomach to see those two kids. I hated them, yet I wanted to be in there, in the photo with them. They had something special that Blindboy and me could never have now. They were safe and warm, protected by something called family love. I knew what that was like. I wanted it back. My craving for it gnawed away inside me.

My dad had loved me when he was alive. When I thought about him I had an empty ache in my chest. Sometimes it actually hurt. Looking at that pic made me miss my dad so much. I smashed the glass, ripped out the pic, and stuffed the frame in my belt.

Just at that moment a soft whistle made the hairs on the back of my neck stand on end. Someone was coming.

I knew I couldn't get to the door in time—now I could hear the footsteps myself—so I quickly ducked behind the far side of the bed.

The footsteps came up to the open door of the apartment, treading warily. Kevin A must have picked up Blindboy and run, leaving me to face the owner of the rooms. I crouched on my hands and knees, ready for flight, and peeked around the edge of the bed. I could see a pair of legs standing in the living room. They looked as if they belonged to an old lady, because they were sheathed in purple stockings and had fusty old shoes on the ends of them.

"Who's there?" cried a shrill voice. "I'm calling the police right now."

However the legs did not move toward the phone and I guessed the old lady was scared stiff. I didn't blame her. She didn't know I was only a kid. For all she knew I could be six feet tall and wielding an iron bar.

I hoped she was kindhearted.

"It's only me," I called in a quavering voice. "I'm coming out, missus. Don't do anything." I got up slowly and walked to the bedroom doorway.

She was between me and the open apartment door. Just as I'd guessed, she was in her sixties, lumpy, with makeup so thick I couldn't see an inch of skin on her face. Eyes bright as blue glass peered out from beneath black-arched eyebrows that had been painted on her forehead. She stared at me. At first her eyes were full of fear, but when she saw the frame in my belt, she gave way to anger.

"That's my photograph," she snapped. "My grandchildren!" She suddenly reached into her evening bag and pulled out a spray can.

"I'll fix you, you little spat!" she hissed, advancing on me with her finger on the button.

I panicked. Without really thinking I quickly reached into my pocket and pulled out my latest carving. I tossed the crudely shaped piece of brown wood at the old lady, hoping to distract her for a moment while I ran past her. It landed on her chest and hung there for a second, caught in the cloth by the rough splinters on the wood, until she brushed it away with a look of utter horror on her face.

She screamed and dropped the can. *"A rat!"* she shrieked, staggering backward.

I rushed past her, through the open doorway and down the stairs to the street.

Kevin A already had Blindboy in the bender with the motor running. I had hardly closed the door behind me before the vehicle jumped forward and screeched around the corner. We hurtled along the street at 120 klicks per hour.

Kevin A's face was white and grim; his eyes constantly flicked to the rearview mirror. I could see the veins on his bony forehead standing out like wires on an ancient circuit board. Only when we were in sight of the warehouse and there were no flashing lights or sirens behind us did he relax a little.

"What did you get, girl?" he asked, stopping outside the warehouse.

I pulled out the jewels and dropped them into his hand.

"Great! That's good, kid. And what's that you've got stuck in your gut?"

"Photo frame," I said, pulling it out. "Silver."

He looked at it carefully and then winced.

"Amalgam," he said in a disgusted tone. "Never mind. The dewdrops will do for one night."

We climbed out of the bender, with Kevin A gripping Blindboy's wrist since the cuffs were off. With his free hand he reached out and ruffled my hair, making me pull away. I hated being touched—especially by a creep like him.

"You did good, girl. Hey, how did you get out of the apartment? You kill the old crow?" He sniggered.

"No," I said, "she got scared by a savage bit of wood that I tossed at her."

"A *what*?" cried Blindboy.

Kevin A looked at me with a puzzled expression and then his eyes opened wide and his face split into his watermelon grin. "I *told* you them damn carvings looked like rats, didn't I? Dogs and cats, you said, but I said rats. I was right, wasn't I? She thought it was a rat?"

"She thought it was a rat," I admitted grudgingly, while Kevin A's maniacal laugh echoed down the street.

6

Two nights later we were out again. This time Kevin A wanted another bender, for a friend, he said. Nothing too flashy that would attract attention. But fast enough to outrun most family models. I figured the new bender was for a holdup.

We cruised in Kevin A's bender, through the neon-lit streets of the city, over bridges with lights like frozen fireworks. There was noise and bustle, people hurrying to and fro, zipcars sliding gently through the night. In the player district there were open-air markets where game machines fizzed and popped, exploded with color and jingles, filling the evening air with noise and excitement.

"Sounds like fun out there tonight," said Blindboy wistfully.

"Yeah," I said, knowing he meant we were prisoners and freedom was just a step away.

Kevin A was ahead of us, though. "Forget it," he said. "I've locked your doors." We continued cruising the streets until finally we came across a dark powerful-looking bender parked outside a frozen-yogurt parlor. It had smoked-glass windows, perfect for us because witnesses couldn't see the people inside the getaway vehicle and identify them later.

"Okay, kids, this is it," said Kevin A. "You two go and look in the window. When the owner comes, get the key tones, Blindboy."

"Can we have a yogurt while we're waiting?" I asked.

"No, you can't," said Kevin A. "Not while you're working. I'll get you one later."

We knew he would forget that promise. He always forgot his promises. Kevin A had no idea about kids and how they resented being promised something that never came.

He let us out of the bender, first threatening to run us over if we tried to make a break for it. Now *that* was one promise we knew he'd keep.

We went over to the parlor window and I stared inside. There were huge tubs of yogurt and colored flavorings on display. I could see raspberry, strawberry, lime, chocolate, pecan, rocky road, banana, and lots more.

"Blindboy," I said, "be grateful for once that you can't see. There's stuff in there that would make you roll over and wag your tail if you was a dog."

"I can *smell* it," he said, licking his lips.

"Frozen yogurt doesn't have a smell."

"Maybe not, but those flavorings do."

I looked across the street at where Kevin A was sitting in his bender, his narrowed eyes on us. Then I glanced at the bender we were going to steal. Something made me stare a little harder. I could see a green light winking slowly on the dashboard, plainly visible even from behind the smoked glass. I couldn't believe it. *The bender had been left unlocked.*

"Blindboy," I whispered, "we don't need you tonight. The driver's forgotten to lock his bender. I can see the green light glowing. We can just jump in and take it."

"What? Okay, let's go."

I made a signal to Kevin A, then dashed forward and opened the passenger door.

"Quick, inside," I said to Blindboy. He jumped in. Then I opened the driver's door and bent down to find the hood release. I was just reaching for it when I felt a tap on my shoulder.

"Blindboy," I said, "leave me alone for a minute. I'm trying to start this zipcar."

Blindboy's voice said, "I never touched you. It was this kerk who's got hold of my arm—"

I jerked upright and peered at the backseat. There beside Blindboy was a thickset man who stared at me with hard black eyes. He was smartly dressed, with a neat haircut, and I guessed straight off he was a cop in plain clothes.

"Going somewhere, girl?" he said in an amused tone.

I threw open the door and leaped out. Not even thinking about Blindboy in my panic, I made off along the pavement, weaving among the knots of people. Before I had gone ten steps I knew that someone was chasing me. Cops always worked in twos and it was the second policeman, standing somewhere out on the street, who was after me.

I headed for the player market, hoping to lose the cop among the machines and players. People were yelling at me as I crashed against them, knocking them off the pavement and into the road. Some of them halfheartedly tried to grab my collar as I dashed past, but the attempts were either too late or too feeble, because I easily brushed them off.

"Out of the way!" I yelled as I ran into the market. "Keep out of my way!"

My breath was raw in my throat now and my chest was heaving with the exercise. It seemed I couldn't get enough air. My legs were beginning to wobble a little.

When I stopped, gasping, to look behind me I could see the cop coming, grim-faced and determined. He looked like one of those square-jawed types who enjoy beating suspects with his bare hands. I could see by his expression that he was not appreciating his exercise either. If he caught up with me I was going to suffer for making him run.

With my chest rattling and heaving, I came out of the player market on the far side. There was a long alley across the street. I ran down this narrow passageway, looking right and left for some exit small enough that I could get through but he couldn't: something like a hole in a fence. Nothing. I sobbed with the effort of drawing breath. The pain in my chest, in my legs, was terrible. All I could find was dark shadows and brick walls. No escape hatches.

The shoes pounded the stone flags of the alley behind me. A quick glance told me that I would at least make it out of the passageway before I was caught.

I came to the end, where I could see bright lights once again. I was just about to take my life into my hands and leap out among the speeding zipcars when one drew up alongside the curb. A window slid down on the driver's side and as I stood there drinking in air like water, the first cop's face appeared. "Going somewhere, girl?" he said again, in that amused tone that made me want to kick him. Then a strong pair of hands clamped onto my shoulders. "I oughta whap you one," gasped the second cop, as his fingers dug into my collarbones. "I'm done in."

The first cop spoke again, his voice hard. "None of that, Phil. The kid was scared—that's why she ran. I won't have any strong-arm stuff."

"A good whapping never hurt any kid for long, Jack," said Phil, his grip loosening a little. "I whap my own kids even. . . ."

"Do you?" said Jack. "Well, you're keeping your hands to yourself while you work with me. Get the girl in here and we'll take 'em to the station. I've been talking to Blindboy here and we seem to have found ourselves an interesting pair of thieves in these two. Let's go."

So that's how we met Jack Rickman, who was a detective sergeant in the police force. Him and Phil Cannigan, who was just a detective, had been staked out by the yogurt parlor, watching an apartment across the street. We had actually tried to steal a police bender, though we couldn't have known it because it had no markings of any kind.

Phil Cannigan wanted to hand us over to the kiddie cops right away; then we would have been sent straight to the sweatrooms. But Jack Rickman, who had listened to Blindboy confessing to being able to hear key tones, said, "Wait a minute, Phil. These kids aren't real criminals. There's something unusual going on—let's get to the bottom of it."

Then Jack turned to me. "What's your part in all this, girl?"

There was something about Jack Rickman that made me want to trust him. Of course, he was a cop, so I didn't want to get carried away. I glanced at Blindboy, who was waiting to hear my answer.

"I can hotwire anything from a shaving razor to a jet aircraft," I told him, not without a touch of pride.

"That's very interesting," said Jack. "Now what about you, Blindboy? You say you can hear ultrasonic tones?"

Blindboy and me were sitting in front of Jack's desk in the police station while he and Phil quizzed us on our backgrounds. I had never been in a police station before—it seemed full of movement and the sound of telephones.

"I'm hungry," said Blindboy, by way of an answer. "Can we have some frozen yogurt?"

Jack said, "When we've finished here I'll take you out for one."

This might have been another promise—just like Kevin A's—but something in Jack's voice made me think he meant it. Phil gave a disgusted snort, but Jack silenced him with a hard look. "Now, what about these tones?" he continued. Then, "No, wait, let's hear how you came to be a dump kid. Hotwire here has told us her dad was killed and she found herself an orphan. What happened to you, Blindboy? Were you born on the dump?"

Blindboy was a very private person. I waited with as much interest as the two policemen to hear what he had to say, because I had never heard the full story.

"My mom and dad were farmers," said Blindboy, "with two children, me and my sister, Em. The banks took away my dad's farm when he couldn't pay the mortgage, so Dad soused the house in kerosene and burned it down. Mom, Dad, and Em stayed inside."

Jack and Phil looked at each other and Phil Cannigan actually winced.

"How come you didn't stay with them, Blindboy?" Jack asked in a quiet voice.

"I got scared," said Blindboy, "when I felt the heat. It hurt. I just ran and jumped out the window and kept on running till I fell over."

"Is that when you . . . lost your sight?"

"No, I was always blind, right from a baby."

"Then," interrupted Phil, "how did you know where the window was?"

Blindboy replied rather scornfully, "Just 'cause I'm blind doesn't mean I'm stupid. I'd lived there since I was born. I knew where every stick of furniture was, where everything was in that house."

"What happened after that?" asked Jack.

64

"Hotwire found me and we got to be friends."

The two policemen looked at me, expecting me to continue the story. I shrugged. "He was wandering along a main road and I thought he'd be killed by some zipcar. So I took him back to the dump with me. Like he said, we got to be buddies. We found out he could hear things everyone else couldn't, electronic things, and we started working together like a team— like you two."

Jack acknowledged this with a nod. "When did you meet this Kevin A?" he asked.

"Just a few weeks ago," said Blindboy, "when he found out we could make tonal keys. He asked us to make one for him."

"Actually," I said, "it was for Mouseman."

Phil's eyes widened and he stared at me. "You know Mouseman?"

"No," Blindboy said, "we don't know him, but we met him once. Kevin A took us to his place. We made a key for him. We didn't know they were crooks then. We only found out later. Then Kevin A said he would send us to the sweatrooms if we told the co— the police. So we didn't. Then Kevin A came to the dump and made us go with him."

"Can you show us where these buildings are, where Kevin A and the Mouseman live?"

"Sure," I said. "After a frozen yogurt?"

"Before," said Phil emphatically.

So they drove us in the police bender, first to the place where we had met Mouseman, and then to the warehouse where Kevin A had kept us prisoners. Both places were empty, but on the drive to the yogurt parlor Jack told us he had expected as much.

"As soon as this character Kevin A suspected you'd been picked up, he would have warned Mouseman and then cleaned out his own place. We won't catch them as easily as this."

He was silent for a few moments, seemingly intent on his driving, before he spoke again. "What I propose to do is this. I'm not going to turn you kids over to the proper authorities. I'm going out on a limb here. I'll keep you with me. You'll sleep at my apartment, with me and Barb. That's my wife. I want you two to help me catch these crooks—not just find them, that's easy enough, but get some proof that will hold up in court."

Phil laughed. "You know what'll happen?" he said. "You'll wake up tomorrow morning and find your TV set missing and these two poor little orphans gone. They'll clean you out, Jack."

Jack gave each of us a quick look. "No they won't," he said. "Basically they're good kids. They've hit hard times, like a lot of people, but they're not thieves at heart. I'm inclined to trust them."

Blindboy's hand crept into mine and squeezed my fingers. I think he was trying to tell me that we should go along with what was happening, so I told Jack that we wanted to help, that we would not steal anything from his apartment, that we would treat his home with respect. He seemed pleased with this response, though I wasn't sure I meant it all. We wouldn't steal anything, but Blindboy and me were no cop's little helpers any more than we were thieves. We wanted nothing to do with either side, cops or crooks.

The yogurt tasted good, though.

7

While we were eating our yogurt I studied the two cops closely. They were at a corner table while we sat at the counter, so it was easy to watch them without being noticed. They were discussing some other case, not connected with me and Blindboy.

Phil was bigger and bulkier than Jack, who was kind of compact. Phil was a wazzootruck, while Jack was a fast bender. And Phil's brain seemed to work more slowly, staying doggedly one-track. He went over things bit by bit, always arriving at the same answer.

"Look, the guy left the wrench under the *bed*, Jack. Who needs a wrench in a bedroom? I think we got to nail him right now, before he does a runner."

Phil's big meaty hands waved in the air as he spoke, the right one moving faster and faster whenever he had a special point to make. His expression was always solid earnestness. You'd think he created the world and never stopped worrying about its future.

Jack was patient with his partner, but you could see his mind was quicker. He was like some fast animal, a fox or wild dog, ready to pounce on prey. He kept his hands flat on the table while he leaned over and considered each detail Phil put to him, shaking his head and giving a sideways smile every so often as if life was full of funny surprises.

"Yes, but Phil," he interrupted his partner quietly, "the guy had an iron-framed bed. Maybe, just maybe, the bolts on the bed came loose and he was tightening them with the wrench?"

Yes, I thought to myself, Jack was definitely the brains of the duo.

After we had eaten our frozen yogurt (I had pecan and Blindboy had rocky road, but we tasted each other's), we were taken to a block of apartments on the west side of the city. I could see from the outside that it wasn't a real swazz place, but it wasn't bad either. Jack was no slummer. It was sort of middle-diddle with few extras.

Jack took us up in the elevator to the third floor. We walked down the passageway until we came to number twelve and then Jack took out a tonal key. He was about to press it when he suddenly stopped and looked at Blindboy.

"Put your fingers in your ears," he said.

Blindboy didn't realize he was being spoken to until I nudged him and he said, "Huh?"

"He wants you to block up your ears," I explained. Blindboy did as he was told and Jack pressed the key, unlocking the door. I nudged Blindboy again and he removed his fingers, but he turned to Jack and smiled. "I can hear anyway," he said smugly, "whether I block my ears or not."

Jack stared at him before opening the door. "You better be on my side, kid," he said.

The apartment was just as I'd imagined, simple furniture but not too old or worn. A woman was there drinking a cup of coffee, and she got up as we came in. Jack walked over to her and kissed her on the cheek. "These are the slummers I told you about on the phone, Barb," he said, pointing to us. I went hot with embarrassment.

"We're no slummers," Blindboy said stiffly. "We've got good shoes on our feet."

The woman named Barb smiled at us. "He's just teasing you," she said. "I can see you're well dressed. Won't you come in? It's rather late, but do you want something to eat?"

Barb was slim, probably a bit younger than Jack, with this sort of round friendly face. When she smiled she showed her gums and her cheeks sort of expanded sideways. I liked her. She didn't wear much makeup and she had short curly hair like me, only better cut.

Jack kept taking hold of her hand and then letting it drop, as if he couldn't help touching her but then remembered there were other people present.

"They've just had two giant-sized frozen yogurts," said Jack, "which is enough for any kid at the end of the day."

Before we could protest, Barb offered us a cup of hot chocolate, which we accepted instantly.

"What's the matter with the boy?" she whispered as she went past Jack into the kitchen, and he murmured, "Blind."

Blindboy gave a little shudder at this. He didn't like people talking about him as if he wasn't there. I gave him a playful punch on the arm, just lightly, and he swung back immediately, catching me in the ribs. After that he was all right again.

"What are your names?" Barb asked, returning with two steaming cups.

"Blindboy and Hotwire," I said, taking a cup.

"I don't have to ask which is which, do I"—she smiled—"but surely you've got *real* names?"

I put the cup into Blindboy's hands.

Blindboy snapped, "Those *are* real names."

She looked at him for a few moments, then said, "Of course they are, I'm sorry. Well, drink up."

Once we drank our chocolate, Barb showed us into a room where there were two camping mattresses on the floor, some blankets, and two pillows. She said, "I'm afraid we've only got the one bed. . . ."

"That's okay," said Blindboy. "That'll do for us."

I nudged him hard.

"The mattresses are fine, Barb," I said. "We're used to sleeping rough anyway. I like the pillows."

Blindboy nudged me back. He knew I was trying to please her and I think he was wondering why. I guess I was thinking that for just one evening maybe, we could be a family—me and Blindboy, and Jack and Barb—like in the pic. We could be kids, really be sister and brother, with real parents to take care of us.

Before I caught myself, I heard myself asking, "Barb, don't you have any kids of your own?"

"That's Mrs. Rickman to you," said Jack, coming up behind her. "And I think that question's off-limits."

"Oh, Jack, don't be so stuffy. Barb's all right. It's my name, isn't it?"

"Bit familiar," grumbled Jack. Then he added, speaking to us, "Don't get up and walk around in the night. There's an alarm system that will go off if you go anywhere except to the toilet across the hall. You got that? No running away."

I grimaced. "Where have we got to run away to?"

"Okay, well, I was just warning you."

We were then forced to have a quick shower by Jack and put to bed by Barb. I started to feel the same ache I got when I saw the old woman's family pic. I fell asleep pretending Jack and Barb were our parents and didn't wake until the next morning.

Barb gave us a big breakfast and then she had to dash off to work in the city hospital. She was a doctor, Jack told us when she'd gone, and from the way he said it he seemed pretty proud.

We went back to the police station, where Phil Cannigan was waiting. "Let's get this thing done," he said grumpily.

He and Jack took us into a room full of electronic equipment, and Jack handed Blindboy a set of headphones. "What we're going to do, Blindboy," he said, "is play you some recordings of telephone conversations."

"What kind of phone conversations?" asked Blindboy. "What should I hear?"

Phil Cannigan seemed to have forgotten that he didn't trust us. He was clearly eager for Blindboy's reaction.

"We've managed to tap the phone lines from Mouseman's residence," he said, "and we have recordings of calls he's made to certain people. Some of them we know, some we don't. Somewhere out there he's got a massive computer center that he uses to steal money from the banks. We want you to listen carefully, to see if you can hear a computer in the background on any of these calls."

"Computers don't use tones," said Blindboy.

"We know that," said Jack, "but you told us you used to find things hidden in the dump—electronic gadgets that let out a sound from their live storage units. Well, a computer must be making a *heck* of a noise—up in the ultrahigh superhigh frequency bands—while it's working. All those chips, resistors, capacitors, live electrical circuits, whatever, crackling and humming away? I mean, *we* can't hear it in the background, over the phone, but *you* might be able to."

"I'll give it a try," said Blindboy.

"Okay," said Phil, "I'll start the recording and you say *stop* when you hear something that you want to tell us about. Okay? The recording will start the minute Mouseman lifts his phone to dial the number. Anyway the first thing you'll hear is what's in the room where he keeps his phone. Now we want you to wear these headphones so you can concentrate, not get distracted by any of the electrical gadgets in this building, but we'll also be listening through the speaker over there." He pointed to a big black box.

Blindboy said, "Got it," and put on the headphones, and Jack started the first recording.

A minute after the click of the telephone receiver

being lifted from the cradle sounded on the speaker, Blindboy shouted, "Stop!"

They stopped the recording.

"Right," said Blindboy. "Somewhere in Mouseman's room is a Xanadu refrigerator with a freezer attachment, a Bolingson electronic cigar lighter, a Smith and Watson burglar alarm system, and a Minaksu coffee-making machine."

I saw Phil's jaw drop and Jack's eyes open wide. Phil said, "You can identify the *brand names* of those things, just from listening to the emissions?"

I didn't know what *emissions* meant but I sure was proud of Blindboy. You could see with half an eye that he had impressed both cops, and it takes a lot to excite a couple of tough policemen who think they know everything. Blindboy had told me that he only had to hear a gadget's circuit noise once to recognize it when he heard it again, like it was a song or something.

"It's not hard," said Blindboy modestly. "I'm an expert at this."

"Well, I'll be," whispered Jack, his voice full of awe.

Once they got over their admiration of Blindboy's talents, they continued playing back the recording. I heard Mouseman's voice asking someone if he had received a package. The person answered that he had and that everything was fine. Blindboy stopped the recording again and gave Jack and Phil a list of all the gadgets and devices he could hear in the background of the person's room.

"No computer, though?" said Jack, in a disappointed voice.

"Yes," Blindboy said, "but as I told you, it's just a small Wenkle PC, for office use, not a big massive thing like you want."

"Okay," Phil said, "let's keep going."

We went through half a dozen more calls, then Jack announced a break for lunch. The two policemen took us up to the canteen, on the sixth floor, where they let us choose what we wanted to eat. We both had Bamwamburgers and Frizzo.

"Don't you kids ever eat any decent food with vitamins in it?" said Jack, pointing to his cabbage. "Your hair will start falling out before you're twenty, you go on eating that trash."

"We like Frizzo and burgers," said Blindboy with his mouth full, "and we probably won't live till we're twenty. Most dump kids die before they're fifteen."

That stopped them in midchew.

"We like burgers too," said Jack after a while, "but not for every meal."

I told him, "We get plenty of vitamin stuff on the dump. They're in the all-mixed-together slop, all the food people chuck away, so there's got to be *everything* in it, including cabbage and stuff like that. Only you can't really tell, because it just looks like a greeny-gray mess."

Phil had been about to take a bite of his sandwich, but he stopped and made a face. "Do you mind?" he said. "I'm trying to eat."

"That's what we're talking about, kids trying to eat," said Blindboy. "They'd starve if there wasn't any slops."

Jack went red and said softly, "There's not much I can do about it, is there? I can't feed the whole city. I got a job to do and I do it. All the homeless kids, running wild in the streets, the poverty. Not just kids. There are old women who die of the cold in back alleys. Old men who drink stuff I wouldn't clean my bathroom with. What can you do? There's too many of them. . . ."

"Can't do anything," I agreed, surprised by the guilty sound in his voice. "What can anyone do?"

Jack shook his head.

"Nothing," said Blindboy. "You just got to look after yourself."

Jack shook his head slowly. "That's no answer."

Well, maybe it wasn't an answer, but it was the only one we kids knew.

After lunch we all trooped back to the recording room and Blindboy started listening to more calls. Finally, late in the day, he came to the one Jack had been waiting for. I could tell because Blindboy's face started to shine, the way it does when he hears a good piece of junk under the dump. He took off his headphones. "That was it, Jack," he said. "Great big monster of a thing in that room. It nearly blew my brains out."

Both policemen became agitated. "You're sure?" said Phil. "Absolutely sure?" said Jack.

Blindboy shrugged. "All I know is there's something huge, using a lot of power, a lot of circuits. Whether it's Mouseman's computer center is up to you to say."

"Got to be it," said Jack happily. "Now we've just got to run that call through the analyzer to get the number he called."

"061–387–6254," said Blindboy.

Phil stared at him. "You knew that?" he asked.

"I know all the numbers Mouseman dialed. I memorized the tones as they went out."

"Damn, you're a genius, kid."

I could have told them that.

8

When we got back to Jack's apartment that evening there was a note from Barb. It said she had to work late at the hospital and wouldn't be home until midnight. He probably got notes like that all the time, doctors being as overworked as they arc, but tonight Jack muttered something to himself, then turned to us.

"Listen, you two, I've got to go out on another surveillance job. You'll have to amuse yourselves in here until either I get back or Barb comes home. On no account are you to leave the apartment, you hear? If you're caught by Kevin A or Mouseman, this operation will be blown sky-high. I can't risk that."

"Can't we come with you?" asked Blindboy.

"No chance," said Jack. "You stay here."

"We wouldn't get in the way," I pleaded.

"I said *no*," repeated Jack. "My superiors wouldn't like it a bit. They don't know I've got you two holed up here and I don't want them to know until we've wrapped this thing up. You watch some television"— he glanced at Blindboy and looked uncomfortable— "that is, Blindboy can listen. There's a laser deck there with some of the latest pop songs, if you prefer that. Just don't have the volume too loud, because of the neighbors. As for food, there's pizza in the fridge. Can you use a microwave oven?"

Blindboy put on a sour expression. "Does the president tell lies?" he said.

"Okay, well, don't go and burn anything. Barb hates bad smells in the kitchen." Jack left us to it then.

Barb and Jack had a puny television set with about a one-meter screen, not one of the modern wall screens that fill the whole side of the room. I didn't even bother to turn it on. Instead we used the laser deck, even though the pop songs Jack mentioned had been off the charts for ages.

Out on the dump we used to find radios all the time and listen to nail music. Jack's *latest* laser discs were at least three months old. I mean, the stuff was ancient.

"You like Meshdriven Minds?" I asked Blindboy, coming up with a barely acceptable band.

"Take 'em or leave 'em."

"Yeah, me too, but it's the best he's got."

"Okay, put it on. What are they doing?" asked Blindboy.

"'Sail the Seven C's.'"

Blindboy shrugged. "Okay, but I heard it a zillion times already."

"Who hasn't!" I triggered the disc and filled the room with sound. Then I pranced around a bit, but I've never been a good dancer. Blindboy's better than me because he just lets himself go and doesn't worry who sees it. I get sort of shy when people are there, and even when they're not.

When the music was over I went to the fridge and got us a pizza each—Jumbo-Giant-Double-Bombers—though I expect Jack intended us to have just a single one between the two of us. I had a seafood Medley-of-the-Ocean and Blindboy chose Symphony-of-Hams. They were so big around, it was difficult to get them both in the two-tier micro, but we did it by trimming the edges with a pair of scissors.

At the sound of the bell, we took out the steaming pizzas and buried our noses. Blindboy surfaced for air after a few minutes. "I could really go for a Frizzo," he said.

"Me too. Trouble is," I remarked, "Jack and Barb don't buy Frizzo. I've been through the fridge and the closest they get is a Chokola. I hate Chokolas."

"So do I," grumbled Blindboy. "What does Jack drink?"

I grimaced. "Milk."

"Milk?" cried Blindboy. "Milk's for babies."

I sighed in sympathy. "Well, it's either Chokola or milk."

"What a choice."

We sat there in silence for a few minutes, not even touching our pizzas anymore. I mean, how can you enjoy something that gives you a raging thirst when you know you can't quench the fire in your throat?

Finally I couldn't stand it any longer. "That's it," I said. "I'm going downstairs. There's got to be a Frizzo machine in the foyer."

Blindboy said, "Jack told us not to leave the apartment."

"Yeah, well, he meant the building. There can't be any harm in just going down to the foyer. I mean, it's all lit up and no one can get inside the street doors unless they live here, can they? I'll die without a drink."

Blindboy still looked unsure about it, and to tell the truth I wasn't sure myself. Maybe Jack *did* mean the apartment itself. Still he wouldn't be happy to come home to two dead bodies on his carpet, dry as husks.

"Well, I'm going," I said. "I've got just enough money for two Frizzos. Shut the door behind me and don't let anyone in without the password."

"What's the password?"

"I love anchovies."

Blindboy laughed. We both hated anchovies.

So I opened the door and slipped out into the hall. I took the elevator to the ground floor and got out. There was a kind of open foyer in all decent apartments where you had a public phone, usually a coffee machine, and often a Frizzo, candy, and potato-chip machine.

Only, there were no Frizzos left.

"Kapitan Kerk, no Frizzos!" I swore at the machine and gave it a bit of a kick.

Just then someone came in through the doors. It was a middle-aged man with some groceries. I went up to him. "You got any Frizzos in there, mister?" I asked. "I can pay for them."

He frowned at me and asked, "What are you doing in here, girl?" He put his groceries on the foyer table and turned to face me. I put on my innocent look. After all, I *was* innocent.

"Nothing. That is, we're living with Jack Rickman, the policeman, and his wife, Barb."

The man put his hands on his hips. "There's no subletting in this block. It's not allowed."

"Hey," I said, "do I look like an adult to you? I'm a guest."

"You look like a street kid to me. What did you kick the machine for? I saw that. You kicked the machine. You trying to get the money out? Eh?"

"Look, mister . . ."

He was really steamed up.

"Anyone can look at the resident listing." He pointed to a board fastened to the foyer wall.

I saw what he was getting at. It gave the names and addresses of the people who lived in the building. "'Mr. John Rickman' and 'Dr. Barbara Rickman,'" I read. "Everyone calls him Jack."

"I don't," replied the man, staring at me with hard eyes. "When I see him I call him *John* and he doesn't bat an eyelid. What do you think of that?"

"Well, his partner calls him Jack and so does his wife."

"Says you. Well, young lady, I think you made a guess and I think you made it wrong. Out. Outside."

He grabbed me by the collar and lifted me off my feet. Before I could kick him or even protest, he had opened the street doors and thrown me through the doorway. I landed on my feet but fell over onto the pavement.

"You kerk!" I yelled. "I'll get Jack to throw you in jail."

I looked around me. People were hurrying by, taking little notice of my dramatic exit. I brushed myself off and took stock. Since I was outside the building I thought I might as well get a couple of Frizzos. At least I wouldn't have to go back to Blindboy empty-handed.

84

I crossed the street to a supermarket and went in. At the fizzy-drinks shelves I grabbed a couple of Frizzos and went straight to the checkout, paid for the drinks, and stepped out on the street.

A shadow fell over me from behind. I was about to turn and see who it was when a hand flashed out and grabbed my wrist. Looking up I found I was staring into a face with thin features, narrow eyes, and a triumphant smile.

The hand that held me was a woman's, but it was as strong as steel. "Got you," she snapped. "I seen your picture."

"Picture?" I cried.

"Kevin A wants you," she said.

"*Help!*" I yelled. "Kidnap! HELP!"

Nobody took any notice. You could get your throat cut on the streets of the city and no one would care.

The woman dragged me over to a phone. She put an armlock around my neck like she was a professional wrestler. Then she took the phone off the hook, dialed a number with the same hand, and waited.

"Kev!" she shrieked into the phone. "I've got the girl. We're on Breeme Street South. . . ."

The woman relaxed a little to get a better grip on the phone so I used this opportunity to bite her arm. She screamed and jerked backward, and I managed to wrench myself from her grasp. I started running. I heard her curse, then start after me. Kevin A had obviously put out a reward for Blindboy and me. When had he taken our pictures? In the warehouse, probably, with a secret camera. He wasn't such a dimsum after all.

I weaved in and out among passersby, leaving some of them cursing and swearing about street kids running wild, but whenever I looked behind, the woman was still after me, a determined look in her eyes.

Kevin A must want us badly. He had obviously offered a lot of reward money for our capture. Why else would a woman out shopping chase me with such eagerness?

Suddenly a bender pulled up alongside the curb. Kevin A and two men came at me, running. I ducked down an entrance to the subway.

When I came to the ticket barrier I jumped over the turnstile like a real athlete. A few people coming through the stiles gasped, but whether at my wonderful leaping or because I wasn't paying remained a mystery to me. I guessed it was probably both.

I took the escalator steps three at a time. It was several seconds before I realized I was running down the *up* escalator. Luckily Kevin A and his pals had followed me instinctively, so we were all going down the same one. Passengers coming the right way were annoyed as I pushed through them. I heard Kevin A yelling, "Stand aside! Escaped lunatic! Stop that kid!"

But just as people didn't want to help me when I

was being abducted by the woman, these people didn't want to help Kevin A. Nobody wanted to get involved. If anyone seemed about to try to stop me, I bared my teeth.

At the bottom of the escalator I turned to Stations West. A train was pulling in somewhere on that side: I could hear the squeal of its brakes and then the doors opening. With my lungs bursting, I ran down three sets of stairs and out onto the platform. The train doors were just closing. I jumped for the nearest one— and just scraped through. I landed in the car next to another young kid, a girl in a fake fur. She looked like a rich kid.

"Hi!" I wheezed. "Nearly missed it. Daddy *would* have been upset. He's a cop, you know."

Her eyes opened wide and then she turned away, ignoring me, clutching at an adult's hand.

Before the train pulled out I saw Kevin A standing on the platform gulping for breath. He stared at me. I waved pleasantly. Then I saw him whip out his pocket phone. The next moment I heard a chirping from somewhere in the car. It might have been a coincidence, but I didn't think so.

Kevin A had recognized someone on the train. He was calling that someone now, telling him or her that I was in there, and to catch me.

9

Whoever was in the car working for Kevin A didn't reveal themselves. That was worse than coming and grabbing me. At least then I could have yelled and made a fuss, hoping someone would come to my rescue. As it was I just had to wait and see what happened. I moved to the part of the car farthest from where I had heard the phone ring and jiggled the connecting door. It was locked, so I huddled into a corner behind some passengers.

The train rattled on to the next station. I stared out the window at the blackness, which occasionally lit up when blue sparks crackled from the live rail. I had already made up my mind to leave the car at the next station, but I had to do it craftily.

When we pulled in and the doors hissed open, I stepped outside and stayed by the doorway, as if I was ready to jump back in again. As the other alighted passengers moved off, I could see no one standing waiting with me. The person with the phone must have been standing just inside the doorway of the car, ready to jump off if I stayed on the platform. I hung around the open doors, trying to give the impression that I was going to jump back on the train just before it pulled out.

Just as the doors began to close I started to move forward as if I was going to leap back on again, but I held back at the last moment. The doors slammed shut. After a few moments the train pulled out.

"Bye-bye!" I called, and waved.

I headed for the exit, but before I was halfway down the platform I realized they had fooled me after all. I figured the person on the train phoned ahead so his cronies could beat the train to the station, and they must have driven here. Two large men were blocking my only exit.

One of them was speaking into the phone in his hand, grinning at me at the same time. The other one beckoned with a finger. "Come on, girlie," he said, "this is the only way out."

I stared at him and then looked around me. I hate being called girlie. I was scared, but I was angry now too. Maybe if I hadn't been so furious I wouldn't have done it.

"You're wrong, kerk," I yelled. "There *is* another way!" And I jumped down into the track bed.

I ran along the tracks, being very careful not to touch the live rail—the underground rail system hadn't yet been converted to skiddertrains and still ran on electricity.

I reached the tunnel at the other end, stopping just to catch my breath. Finally, with my throat as dry as dust, I plunged into the black gaping mouth of darkness.

Once inside the tunnel I was really scared. A feeling of misery came over me and I knew I was missing Blindboy. When the two of us were together we could cope with anything. Now I was on my own. I knew how easy it was to trip in the darkness and fall onto the live rail. I didn't want to fry like an egg, so I slowed my pace and began to walk carefully, keeping one hand on the dusty wall. That way I kept my balance and my distance from the left side of the tunnel. I knew the live rail was just ten centimeters or so from my right foot.

After a while I found it easier to hold one of the cables that ran along the tunnel wall. It helped me feel more secure in my balance. The only thing was that rats ran along the cable and kept skittering over my hand. I was used to rats at the dump, but I still didn't like them much. It's crazy to jerk your hand away, though, because that's when they bite you, when they sense a sudden movement. As long as you keep still, you're okay. So I let the rats use me as a bridge and tried hard not to think about them.

After a while I stopped for breath. That's when I heard something that made my skin prickle.

Footsteps behind me.

Now it had turned into a race. All I need now is for a train to come along, I thought.

But it wasn't the noise of a train that made me stop in my tracks and shiver. It was a low rumbling sound that gradually grew into a deep-throated growl. Us humans weren't the only big creatures using the underground tunnels. There was something down here just as big.

"What's that?" I yelled.

There was an answering snarl, only this time from a different place.

Just at that moment my fingers found a handle near the cable I was using to guide me. I don't know why I pulled it, but suddenly the tunnel lit up for a hundred meters. I'd found one of the maintenance lights used by the men who repaired the tracks.

Bright eyes shone at me from hunched dark shapes lying all the way along the edges of the tunnel.

Wild dogs! No doubt the rats had attracted the creatures underground. The pack could feed on rats and mice in the tunnels and never have to surface.

The only thing was, I had to get past them.

Just then the lines started rattling violently below my feet as a rush of air whooshed down the tunnel. A train! I flattened myself against the wall as best I could, letting the rats run over my head. Their claws kept catching in my hair, but I had to let them free themselves: I couldn't move my arms. If I had, my elbows would have stuck out in the path of the train.

Ahead of me, on both sides of the track, the dogs hunched themselves against the walls, having learned from experience to get out of the way. Those that hadn't were probably dead. In fact I could see lumps of bones in the dim maintenance lights. A crushed skull there, its eyeless sockets pointing straight at me; a leg and rib cage here, not far from my feet.

I didn't have time to worry about these underground decorations, however; the noise got louder and louder until it sounded as if the train was inside my head. Then suddenly it was on me. It thundered and screamed past, whipping my clothes around in a hurricane of wind, noise, and light.

Dust and grit flew up in clouds, choking me. I could feel the steel wheels of the train hissing by my legs, just centimeters away. The vibrations jolted my whole body, threatening to shake me loose from my hold on the wall. At the same time the wind sucked at me, trying to tear me from my safety and throw me under those wheels. My hair was lashed backward and forward, thrashing my ears and cheeks. I gagged as I fought for oxygen, because the train was dragging all the air along with it.

Then suddenly the noise faded, the pulling sensation ceased, and the tunnel became silent. It was gone as quickly as it had appeared.

I hoped the man behind me had been so scared by the experience that he'd turned back. It had certainly frightened me. I was still shaking and clinging to the wall.

The low growling started again now.

I wanted to go on, but there seemed to be no way I could climb over the dogs without getting torn to bits. The only way past them was to go down the center of the track. Now that the lights were on, I could do that without stepping on the live rail, but what if another train came along?

I looked around. The maintenance lights had to be in this part of the tunnel for a reason and I soon discovered what that reason was. A black box was fastened to the wall just a few meters behind me. I went back to it and undid the dirty fly screw that held down the lid. Inside the box was a mass of wires and junction points and on the other side of the lid, a wiring diagram. I studied the diagram for a few seconds, then knew what I had to do.

"They don't call me Hotwire for nothing," I said to the dogs. "You watch this." I began tugging at leads, disconnecting wires. As I was working, the lines started rumbling again and I knew another train was on its way.

My hands worked feverishly. I didn't want to go through having another train rush past. If it did, I was going to lie down flat by the rail, like the dogs. The suction must not be so bad down there. The noise of steel on steel, though, would be a lot worse, and my ears were already ringing.

Nearer and nearer it came. I began pulling wires out by the handful, wondering if I was right about the box.

Now I could feel the rush of air that preceded the train. I figured I had about three seconds before it would be on me. There were two bunches of wires left.

One second.

I made a quick decision and grabbed the right-hand bunch and wrenched them out.

A bright fountain of sparks spurted from the board as the ends of the wires touched each other—obviously something I had been trying to avoid. I felt the jolt of electricity going through my body. Even though I wasn't touching anything metal at the time, the force was enough to lift me off my feet.

The shock threw me backward, into the middle of the track. I landed on the live rail just as the train came around the bend, its wheels screeching, trailing a stream of sparks. I could smell the odor of steel sliding against steel. I watched as the train got bigger and bigger, hurtling toward me, and finally stopped— one meter from my head.

Soaked in sweat, I climbed unsteadily to my feet. I realized I must have chosen the right bunch of wires at the last moment, because the live rail was dead before I landed on it. Pulling out the wires had saved me in more than one way.

Once I had gathered myself together and stopped trembling, I began walking down the middle of the track. It was safe now that the rail was dead. Luckily the dogs did not know this and kept to the walls of the tunnel, snarling and growling at me as I passed, slinking along the edge of the track, but not willing to risk coming out after me. I guessed they must have thought I was an angel or something, able to tread where they did not dare. Their hackles raised and their teeth bared, all they could do was to snap at air.

Just before the light ran out, I came to a fork in the tunnel. The two tracks obviously led to two different stations. I wondered which one to choose.

Deciding on the right fork I slipped into the blackness again, hoping I would find no more dogs. I could no longer hear footsteps behind me and hoped I had at last shaken off whoever was after me. Suddenly the lights of the next station were glinting on the track. I knew I had made it.

Once I reached the platform I pulled myself up.

Several startled grunts and some pretty hard stares came in my direction. Passengers were not used to seeing a kid come out of the darkness of the tunnel and climb onto the platform.

"S'okay, folks," I said, showing off to the crowd. "I got lost, but I found my way home again."

"That's true enough, girl," said a familiar voice. "You're home all right."

And I felt a hand clamp itself on my shoulder.

10

When I was able to look up I could see this big man with a brutish face looking down at me. He was holding me by the back of the neck and his grip hurt. Standing just a few feet away was the undersized master criminal himself, Mouseman. He looked about ready to eat my head whole.

"Ow," I said. "Tell him not to hold me so tight, Mouseman."

At the sound of the name several people moved away from us. Any help that might have come from that quarter quickly melted away. I kicked myself mentally for opening my mouth.

"Joe," said Mouseman to the gorilla, "ease up."

The fingers on my neck relaxed, but his other hand grabbed me and held me securely. Mouseman nodded to Joe and I was frog-marched out of the station. A stretch skidder was waiting outside and I was thrown without ceremony onto the backseat. Mouseman joined me, and the gorilla climbed into the driver's seat. He was so heavy and bulky the whole vehicle lurched as he squeezed himself behind the wheel. A cop had thrust a parking ticket in the slot provided by law at the windshield. Joe simply picked it out, crumpled it up, and dropped it onto the pavement.

"That's illegal," I said. "Destroying a parking ticket *and* littering the pavement."

Joe turned awkwardly in his seat, his great bulk making the vehicle squeak on its springs. "You want to add murder to that list?" he said gruffly.

I stared at his large bent nose and gulped. "No."

"Then shuddup, or I'll crush your skull like a walnut." I did the wise thing and closed my mouth tightly.

Mouseman said, "Put your head between your knees, girl."

"Huh? What for?" I said.

"Just do as you're told. I don't want you to see where you're going and I can't be bothered to blindfold you. So put your head down, keep it there, and stare at the floor."

"Yes*sir*," I replied, doing as I was told.

Joe drove us to a house out on the edge of the city. I could tell that because even though I couldn't see much, the noise of the traffic lessened the farther we went and I was aware that the bright lights had been left behind. Finally the skidder pulled up and I was told I could look.

We were outside a big house with trees all around and a long driveway behind us. We weren't in the country, because I could still hear the faint roar of the traffic, but at a huge house on the edge of the city. I guessed we were on the stockbroker belt. The house was a mansion, almost a palace. I'd never seen one like it and it must have shown on my face.

Mouseman turned and looked at me and when he saw my expression he laughed. He was used to giant estates like this. I'd heard on the streets that Mouseman's family had once been very powerful, a big name in politics and business. Then his father had been pulled in on corruption charges, accused of skimming charity funds, bribing voters, and various other crimes. The family was ruined, with Mouseman emerging from the wreckage to begin his own chosen career in the world of crime.

Joe came and dragged me from the backseat while I was still gaping at my dark surroundings. He carried me into the house and through a large hallway with a great staircase curving upward, out a door at the back and into the kitchen, then down a long flight of stone steps to the cellar below. Joe went behind some wine vats at the back and pressed a wet stone in the wall, and one of the vats tipped up to reveal another flight of stairs.

We went down these and into a world of bright lights and technology. Technicians moved back and forth, quietly and without any fuss, twiddling knobs and turning handles, working keyboards and little micromice on gray pads. Lights flashed, dimmed, went out, and came on.

There, in the center of the massive underground complex, was Mouseman's giant computer. I was in the core of his empire. It was here he embezzled millions of macrobucks, controlled companies and funds, and managed his criminal empire. This was Mouseman's master hole. I was staring at this great device as Mouseman came into the room. He must have seen the glow of satisfaction on my face.

He said, "I know what you're thinking, girl, and let me put your mind at rest. No one will come here to rescue you. You believe that fool Rickman has discovered the whereabouts of this operation—"

My face must have fallen a little for he smiled grimly.

"—which is not true. I was aware that my telephone was bugged, of course, and purposely made a call to the control center of the subways. They have a similar computer complex, to manage their vast network of trains. It was the subway's computer that the blind boy heard, not *my* machine. Rickman does not have this address and you, you little traitor, are lost forever."

"What are you going to do with me?" I asked.

"First I will use the fact that I have you to get the blind boy in my hands."

"Then?"

He shrugged. "Then I shall invite Joe to get rid of you both. He quite enjoys that sort of thing, don't you, Joe?"

The gorilla smiled, showing only his top teeth.

"You won't get away with it!" I yelled.

Mouseman, the top of his head only at my shoulder, just laughed out loud.

"Of course I shall. Who do you think cares about a couple of kids—*dump* kids—in this day and age? Children like you die on the street every day, and no one gives a hoot. Decent citizens regard you more as pests, as vermin, than they do as fellow human beings. It's sad, girl, but it's true. No one would blink an eye if you turned up dead in the gutter tomorrow."

"Jack Rickman cares!" I yelled.

Mouseman sneered. The fatherly tone I had once heard from him was history. He used his true voice now and it had an evil sound to it. "Jack Rickman? He's one of the worst. He's only using you to get at me. Once you're out of the way and of no use to him anymore, he'll forget you. Don't you understand, girl,

101

Rickman and I have been at war for two decades now? I'm his obsession. As for you? He couldn't care less about you."

Tears stung my eyes. I couldn't believe what Mouseman was telling me. I *liked* Jack Rickman and he liked me. Yet . . . yet I knew there was *some* truth in what I was being told.

"Well, we'll see," I shouted. "We'll just see."

"In the meantime," said Mouseman with a yawn, clearly bored with me now, "we shall inform Rickman that if he doesn't deliver the blind boy into our hands, he'll find your body floating in the river within forty-eight hours. We'll contact him through the media. He won't dare refuse or there'll be an uproar."

I gritted my teeth and clenched my hands. "You do what you like," I said weakly.

"In the meantime," he continued, "you'll stay down here. You're free to wander around. In that office over there"—he pointed to his left—"you'll find a machine that dispenses food and drink. Help yourself, girl. If you touch anything else, you'll be bound and thrown into a closet, so my advice is, *don't*. Make the most of your last few hours of freedom. I won't change my mind about getting rid of you, you know. I believe in punishment. You betrayed me and you'll pay for that betrayal."

Mouseman picked up a pen and snapped it in two with only three stubby fingers of his left hand. "That's what happens to traitors' spines," he said, his lightbulb eyes glinting wickedly.

"How do you figure I betrayed you?" I said stubbornly. "I didn't promise anything to you. It's not betraying anyone if you didn't say you'd be loyal to begin with, is it?"

"I expect loyalty from those I work with, whether I'm promised it or not," he replied. "You and the blind boy will be punished. I've made up my mind about that. I shall also deal with that idiot Kevin A for bringing you to me in the first place, but that can wait. Let him think he got away with annoying the Mouseman for a few weeks."

"Loyalty should go both ways," I said.

The silent gorilla gave me a quick clip on the head for that remark.

Before Mouseman trotted away, with Joe at his heel, he called over a technician with goofy teeth and a weedy body.

"Tweedle," said Mouseman to the technician, "I'm making it your job to watch this girl. If she steps out of line, don't have any hesitation: Knock her back in again. She's your personal responsibility. You understand me, Tweedle? If anything goes wrong and this girl is at the bottom of it, you're the one who's going to hang."

Tweedle's eyes flicked from me to Mouseman and back again. He looked overworked, harassed, and worried. I immediately felt sorry for him. I could see he was the kerk they used for all the dirty jobs.

"Yes, Mr. Mouseman," Tweedle answered. "I'll look after her, sir."

"Good."

After Mouseman had gone I told Tweedle I was hungry and thirsty and he took me to the dispensing machine. I had sausage, fries, and green peas, washed down with a Frizzo. While I ate, I looked furtively around the room for a phone. If I could just get a call out to Jack Rickman! There wasn't a phone in sight, though.

"Tweedle," I said at last, "aren't there any phones down here?"

He smiled his goofy smile. "Nope. We have the computer network. No need for a phone."

I nodded casually, as if I didn't really care.

"But," he continued, "if you're thinking of trying to get a call out, you'll be disappointed. You need a code word to access outside lines and you're not going to get it, are you?"

I shrugged as if I couldn't give a smiff.

"Come on," said Tweedle anxiously after a few minutes. "Finish that up and come with me. I've got work to do."

Curious about what Tweedle's work might be, I finished the Frizzo and followed him to a terminal on one of the computers. A panel had been removed from above the keyboard, revealing a cluster of wires. A great mass of circuit boards, chips, and other gubbins spilled out like the innards of a gutted animal.

"You sit there," said Tweedle, pointing to a swivel chair nearby, "and don't move."

I did as I was told, watching him call up a huge circuit diagram on a second screen. It seemed to be a map of the exposed wiring above the keyboard. Tweedle fussed over this diagram while he studied the tangle of wires. From time to time he pulled out a lead or replaced a board as he found his way through the computer's minijungle.

I watched him working for a while, then studied the rest of the computers in the room. Again I had that funny feeling inside, wishing Blindboy was with me. If he *had* been, we could've taken this place apart. We were a great team, me and him, and there was none to beat us when it came to electronics.

I stared around me. Other circuit diagrams showed on various screens around the room, though none of the other technicians had their panels open. One diagram in particular caught my attention. It seemed to be a plan of the city, with various points marked on the map.

The marks were in the shape of lit red bulbs. One was at City Hall, another at the main police station, another beneath a bridge spanning the river, one more at the largest office building. There were quite a few in all. No one was sitting at this particular terminal, but what struck me as odd was that these places would have terminals coming off Mouseman's computer.

Around the panel of this particular terminal were various warning notices:

TOP CLEARANCE LEVEL ONLY.
MOUSEMAN'S PERSONAL AUTHORITY
IS REQUIRED FOR ACTIVATION OF
THIS TERMINAL. ALL UNAUTHORIZED
TECHNICIANS KEEP AWAY.

Above the terminal was a red handle.

This was a really strange setup. I decided to find out what it was all about.

I turned back to Tweedle. "Black simplex wire to the left side of the blue duplex," I said to him.

He looked up. "What are you talking about?" he asked.

"I just told you. That's why you're not getting any power on the third board."

Tweedle straightened his skinny body and glared at me. "I'll have you know I'm an expert technician," he said.

I replied, "So am I. Why do you think they call me Hotwire?"

"You're just a young girl."

"I'm not *just* a young girl. I'm also a whiz kid with

the wires. Put the black simplex wire in the left blue duplex socket and see what happens."

He stared at me for another second, but he must have been having a lot of trouble, because not only did he look frustrated, tired, and upset, but he finally did just what I'd suggested.

Immediately a row of green GO lights sprang to life on the board.

"What do you know!" he said, stepping back in surprise. "You were right, girl."

"Of course I was right. . . ." I then proceeded, after studying the diagrams further, to tell him where his other problems lay. After a brief series of small arguments he began to follow my instructions to the letter, and we soon had the whole panel back in working order.

"You're brilliant, kid," he said.

"A genius," I replied.

He nodded slowly. "Yes, I suppose you are."

"Listen, Tweedle," I said. "I also noticed a red light flashing on that panel over there, the one with all the warning notices. Does that mean anything?"

He jerked his head around quickly. "What?" he croaked, his eyes wide with fear. "Not the bomb terminal?"

"Nah," I said, smiling. "Just kidding you."

He seemed to collapse a little, and sweat shone on his face. "Good grief," Tweedle whispered, "you don't joke about half a city being blown to smither-eens."

"No," I said, trying to look contrite, "I'm sorry. I didn't realize. Anyway, where am I supposed to sleep? I'm tired. . . ." Now that I had the answer to my question about the mysterious panel, I wanted to think about it. That computer terminal was a terrorist device. Mouseman had wired the city, planted bombs under all the main government buildings, and no doubt would use them one day if he had to. This new piece of information required some real thought.

I had to get out of the cellar somehow.

11

Tweedle led me to a swazz dormitory where aluminum-frame bunk beds lined the walls. They looked comfortable enough, with a blanket and pillow on each of them. The room itself had a pleasant, controlled temperature. I knew I would have to keep pinching myself once I lay down, because I didn't want to fall asleep.

"You can take that one," he said, pointing to a lower bunk at the far end of the dorm.

"Thanks, Tweedle," I said. "A little sleep before dying."

He blinked at me and sucked his teeth. "What do you mean?" he asked.

"I mean Mouseman's going to kill me as soon as he catches my friend Blindboy."

Tweedle blinked again. "He wouldn't hurt a child."

"Says you. He'd murder his *own* baby if it meant more money in the bank."

Tweedle shook his head. "I don't believe you."

"Okay," I replied, amazed at his innocence, "you wait and see."

Before I lay down on the bed, Tweedle took something out of one of the filing cabinets in the corner of the room. It was a set of electronic handcuffs. He clamped them on my wrists, making sure the connecting chain was looped around the bed frame.

"Hey!" I yelled.

"Now you be quiet," said Tweedle. "I want to get some sleep. I've been on my feet for sixteen hours. Just behave yourself. And don't try any tricks with my colleagues. I'm the only one who knows the combination to this." I looked down at the minikeypad on the cuffs. I could press numbers until doomsday and never find the right sequence. It was a slummer.

Tweedle went off somewhere while I fought to stay awake. I dug my nails into the palms of my hands to stop myself from closing my eyes and drifting off.

Despite my casual attitude in front of Tweedle, I was scared. I knew that Mouseman wouldn't hesitate to murder both me and Blindboy if it served his purpose. My time was limited.

Jack Rickman would not give up Blindboy right away, but there might come a time when he felt it necessary. If Mouseman threatened to blow up City

Hall, for example, unless Blindboy was turned over to him. Jack would then have to weigh the importance of several hundred government leaders against the life of two dump kids. I knew who he would have to save.

As I lay there technicians began to drift into the dorm in ones and twos and bed themselves down. Eventually Tweedle came in, took a glance at me and satisfied himself I was secure, and went to sleep. After about an hour or so the room was almost full of sleeping people. I figured they were now all in bed.

With my heart thumping in my chest I looked around in the half-light of the dim lamps. A man was snoring just inches away from me. There was a bedside locker by his head and I could just reach over and gently pull open the drawer—nothing but writing materials, soap, and toothpaste. Then I noticed the nail file. I picked it up carefully, at full stretch on my chain, then tried to pick away at the cuffs. The only thing I succeeded in doing was digging out one of the number buttons, leaving a tiny hole in the keypad. Eventually I gave up.

Next I tried the locker itself, but there was nothing of any use to me, even when I got the door open.

I began to panic a little. Somehow I had to get free of the cuffs and find a way out of the center. I looked around the room.

There was a small electric lamp on the floor near the middle of the room—one of the night-lights. It was too far away to reach with my hands, but I found if I lay down and stretched my legs way out, I could reach it with my toes. I had to try a couple of times before I managed to pull it close enough to pick it up with one hand.

I pulled the wires free of the lamp. Now I had some live electricity to play with. It was a dangerous business and I stood a good chance of electrocuting myself, but what else could I do? Holding the plastic-covered wires, I shoved the live ends through the hole in the cuffs' keypad. There was a fizz, some sparks, and a whirring sound. Luckily the bracelets were insulated and I wasn't instantly fried. I pulled the wires out quickly and looked around. Tweedle grunted and turned over in his bed, but no one else moved at all.

I tugged at the cuffs. My heart sank. They were still locked.

This time I shoved the wires deep in the hole, right into the electronic guts of the handcuffs. They responded by crackling fiercely and getting hot, burning my wrists a little. I kept tugging the whole while until finally they snapped apart. They fizzed a bit more and then the rest of the room lights went out. I had shorted them. My heart pounded.

In a few moments they flicked on again as a trip switch somewhere resumed its normal ON position—

no doubt after the circuit had tested itself and found nothing but a dead lamp.

Rubbing my aching wrists, I made my way across the room, passing Tweedle, who was fast asleep, his goofy front teeth chattering as he breathed.

Once I was out of the dorm I made my way along well-lit corridors to the place where we had entered the computer center. When I found it I searched for the switch that would flip the wine vat trapdoor. After an hour or so, I gave up. Wherever it was, it was too well hidden for me to find.

Well, I wasn't just going to lie down again. I went back to the computer rooms to see what I could discover there.

One thing about technicians is they're generally an untidy bunch of people. They leave their tools lying everywhere. All I needed was a set of screwdrivers, which I found as easy as anything.

For the next hour I messed around, always with an eye to escape. Among other things I tried to get a computer to tell me the location and code of the key to get out of the computer center, but though I've always been swazz at hardware, I'm only so-so at software. I can do things with software but not as well as I can find my way through a bird's nest of wires and electronic components.

Finally I gave up on the computers and concentrated

on the cables instead. Among the manuals on the shelves I found the cable diagram for the whole network. I found what I was looking for and tore out a big fold-up chart.

Then I got down on the floor and began unscrewing bolts and removing duct covers, following the cables out of the room and along the corridor. The cable I was most interested in was a thick black one with a red stripe down one side and a yellow stripe down the other. This snaking monster was the main power cable for the whole computer center and had to come in from the main grid—from the *outside*.

I finally reached a wall at the end of the corridor. There, an old sewer went under the wall, carrying inside it several transmission lines as well as the main power cable. The sewer was not used for waste anymore, but as a makeshift cable duct.

I stared down into the black hole, my heart pattering in my chest. It looked barely big enough to take my body. What if I crawled along that narrow tunnel and got stuck? I would die of thirst or starvation or maybe asphyxiation: a horrible death. Then again, what choice did I have? If I stayed where I was, Mouseman was going to kill me anyway.

I wished Blindboy was with me. I always felt a lot braver when he was there. Somehow just thinking of him gave me the courage I needed.

I got to my feet and dashed back down the corridor,

found a tool bag, and rooted through it till I found what I wanted: a penlight, used for looking in dark corners of computer innards. It had a digital watch on the other end. It said 02.05 hours.

There was one more thing I had to do before I left the computer center, even though it was risky. I hurried back to the mainframe and took off a particular panel. Then I began rerouting wires inside, connecting boards to new locations, and finally, when the hardware was altered, I went into the software and changed that too. Then I replaced the panel so no one would know I'd been inside this particular part of the computer.

I ran back to my hole and crawled down. Unfortunately, since I went headfirst and there was no space to turn around, I couldn't replace the panel behind me, so they would know where I'd gone, but at least I was bound to have a few hours' head start on them.

I kept my arms out in front of me with the penlight shining, lighting the way ahead. The tunnel was dark and dusty, full of spiders and beetles, but at least it was dry. I wormed my way along, wriggling my hips to move forward, using the cables to pull myself down the long dark channel. Cobwebs stuck to my face and got in my nose and mouth, and the dust was choking me.

After twenty minutes of squeezing along the tunnel, I was exhausted. The duct was hot, stifling, and airless. If I stayed still for any length of time I would probably use up the air around me and suffocate.

My knees were chafed raw from rubbing against the tunnel and my hands had blisters on them. Still, I had to keep going, and I kept my eyes open for an opening that might lead me to safety.

Once or twice the duct narrowed for some reason, probably due to problems with the land outside, and I got stuck. I panicked at first but I found if I just stayed still, breathed deeply for a few minutes, and allowed myself to sweat, I could slip forward by fractions and get myself out of trouble.

Finally the duct opened up into a large circular tunnel. I looked at the time. It was 02.35. It had only taken me thirty minutes to crawl down the duct, though it had seemed like hours.

I could tell by the stink what the tunnel was for. It was obviously a sewer and the power cable and computer lines ran along its wall, just above the walkway. I wondered why Mouseman didn't use the phone lines for his computer connections, but when I thought about it I realized he needed his most important terminals hardwired into a private network for security.

For over two hours I walked along the sewer. Finally I came to a fork. I took the left one—maybe it would be luckier for me than that right one in the train tunnel—and continued my underground journey, until at last I arrived at a point where one of the computer lines left the main mass and joined the outside world. Obviously it led to a terminal.

I suppose I should have kept going a while, hoping to find where the main power cable surfaced. That way I would be sure of finding myself in a cable station, among people who had no connection to Mouseman.

However, I was so choked with dust, so tired, so fed up with swallowing cobwebs, I was not thinking straight and wanted to surface as soon as I could.

I crawled along the duct, which left the sewer at right angles and was just as tight as the first one. It led to a panel similar to the one I'd used to escape from Mouseman's computer center. Unable to undo the screws since the heads were on the other side, I punched the panel with my fist until it was loose. Then squirming into a better position, I smashed it with my elbow, and air rushed into the duct. I gulped it down gratefully.

Pushing the rest of the panel away with my hands, I now began to slip through a square exit into what I guessed was some sort of room. The light was out. Once I was in I switched on the penlight and found I was in a cellar. I took the stairs up to the door. It was unlocked.

Opening the door, I crept into a hallway. I'd begun sneaking along the passage when a door was flung open and a light went on.

It was time to run.

I opened the front door just as someone yelled something about stopping and I hit the street with my legs pedaling. I flew along the road. I would run all the way to my home on the dump. There at least I had friends. There I hoped to find Blindboy again. All I wanted now was to be left alone with him.

12

Once I had reached the outskirts of the city I slowed my pace.

I was fed up with cops and crooks. Mouseman, Kevin A, Jack Rickman—they could all go to Mars as far as I was concerned. It was the dump life for me.

Of course I was still concerned about Blindboy, but I figured Jack Rickman would let him go once I got a message to him that I was free. The cop had already given us his word he wouldn't send us to the sweatrooms.

So I went straight back to the dump, where the kids were still rooting around in the rubbish. "Hi, Fridge. Hi, Tin Can. Hi, Zipper," I called to them as I saw them. I even called hi to Oilslick. They looked up briefly from what they were doing, called hi back, then went on with their search amid the trash.

It was as if I'd never been away. To these kids, the world was just the same as a few gray weeks ago. It didn't mean anything to them that I had been missing for all that time. What did it matter? Or that Blindboy was still missing. We could have been dead for all anyone cared.

I knew one thing: that I would go through fire for Blindboy. I worried about Blindboy. I knew that Blindboy worried about what happened to me. Were we the only two people in the world to look out for each other?

I was just rooting around in a pile of trash, wondering how I was going to get Blindboy back, when I noticed three figures coming up over the plateau's edge. It was Kevin A flanked by two heavy-looking men: the same two kerks that had driven away the zipcars me and Blindboy had stolen for Kevin A. I had no doubt who they were coming to get.

I could have made a run for it, but I was tired of running. Instead I stood my ground, feeling defiant, ready to take on whatever Kevin A had to offer.

He stopped a few meters away and put his hands on his hips. "You're causing me a lot of trouble, girl, and I'm beginning to wonder whether you're worth it. You're coming with me."

"I'm not," I said, ignoring his threatening tone.

A second later, Fridge was at my side. "What's the trouble, Hotwire?" he asked.

Kevin A poked a finger at him. "You run away and play, fatso, unless you want trouble."

Now *fatso* is not the word you want to use with Fridge, who is big but mostly muscle. He glared and gave out a long, low whistle. Suddenly kids were coming from all over the dump and gathering around us. I noticed they had each picked up something on the way over: one had a bottle in his hand, another a chunk of rock, another a piece of metal from a skidder motor.

Dump kids have a nose for trouble on their patch and within a minute Fridge and fifty or sixty kids were milling around me, keeping Kevin A and his muscle men away from me.

"You were sayin'?" said Fridge to Kevin A. "Somethin' about me being *fat*?"

"Get out of our way," growled Kevin A, stepping forward and whipping out a laser knife. "Somebody's going to get cut."

The kids all hooted like owls at this remark. Missiles suddenly flew through the air and rained on Kevin A and his two cronies. They hunched down to protect themselves, swearing at us. I saw the laser knife go spinning from Kevin A's grasp as a piece of wood struck him on the wrist.

"Hey!" yelled Kevin A. Suddenly he was no longer

121

the big man handing out orders. There was real fright in his face as he was confronted by a horde of sixty wild and screaming dump kids.

Kevin A's comrades retreated to the edge of the dump, out of range of the missiles. Tin Can and Blow-fly had by this time fixed up a catapult by wrapping a giant rubber belt from an industrial machine around two metal posts. They fitted rocks into the band and fired them at the two muscle men. One was knocked clean over the edge of the plateau. The other crouched down behind the wreck of an old bender.

Kevin A tried to struggle forward through the hail of cans, bottles, and pieces of junk. A bottle caught him behind the ear and knocked him sideways. The kids all gave a big cheer as he staggered away to join his friend behind the dumped bender.

My pals had saved me. They had come to my rescue. They *did* care about me and one another after all. When it came down to it, a threat to one was a threat to all.

When the excitement had died down and we were just standing around talking about it all, Kevin A and his two men returned—this time in handcuffs. They looked sullen and disheveled. There were at least two black eyes among them. Leading them were Jack Rickman, Phil, and Blindboy.

"Blindboy!" I yelled.

I ran to him and hugged him, right there in front of everyone.

Blindboy shrugged me off, a little embarrassed, but he was obviously pleased to be back.

"Hey, you yerky kerk, take it easy," he said.

"Are you all right?" I asked him.

He said, "I'm okay, but what about you?"

"Ahhhh," I said. "Yeah, I'm swazz."

Jack Rickman stepped forward then. "We're going to charge these men with kidnapping, attempted kidnapping, and theft, among other things."

"Okay." I replied cautiously, because I could tell he had something else to add to this speech.

Jack stared at me, making me feel uncomfortable, then said, "That lead Blindboy gave us, on Mouseman's computer center? It turned out to be a subway station."

"I know," I said. "I've been to the real place. Mouseman held me prisoner there. I managed to escape."

Phil nodded. "What we want from you, Hotwire, is the location of Mouseman's computer center."

"I know where it is," I said, "but what do I get for the information?"

"You don't want to help us?" Jack said, looking disappointed.

Blindboy said, "Help *you*? What Hotwire means is

we've been yanked around all over the place, by crooks and cops both, for the last few weeks, and where has it got us? Nobody even bothers to thank us for anything. We live on a dump. We've got nothing, not even a roof over our heads. When is somebody going to help *us*?"

Jack looked unhappy. "Well, I appreciate what you've done for us so far, but what else can I do?"

"How about finding us a real home," I said, "and then I'll show you where Mouseman is. We don't want much. You could . . . well, that is . . . maybe we could come live with you, Jack?" I watched his eyes take on a distant look. "You and Barb. I mean, we wouldn't get in the way or anything. It'd be like, you know, *family*."

His expression wasn't encouraging. He sighed deeply. "Wouldn't work, Hotwire. It's not that I don't like you kids—I think you're great, both of you. It's just, well, Barb and I aren't used to children. We're both career people. You've seen that. We'd all be at each other's throats in a couple of weeks, I just know it. What about you, Blindboy, what do you say?"

Blindboy licked his lips and said, "Sorry, Hotwire, I'm not so stuck on your idea either. I think we just want to be able to help ourselves, that's all. I don't want to be somebody's kid. What I want is for the two of us to be together, but earning our own keep somewhere."

124

So that was it. I had all these pretty pictures in my head of being a family. Still, if Blindboy was against it too, that was it. I couldn't fight both of them.

I swallowed hard and said quietly to Jack, "Okay, you heard Blindboy. That's what we want. Nothing more than that, Jack. To be able to help ourselves. You must know lots of people, Jack. You must know someone we could work for, someone who would pay us so we could live like everyone else."

Jack stood there for a long time, his face creased in thought, then said, "Come with me now. I know what you can do, but we've *got* to catch Mouseman first."

13

Kevin A and his cronies were delivered to the city prison, to be held there until the trial. Blindboy and me went with Jack and Phil to the police station. Upstairs the two cops talked to the chief of police, who kept nodding and looking past them at us two as we sat at Jack's desk, drinking Frizzos. Jack's office wasn't exactly swazz, but the chairs were pretty comfortable. Finally the chief gave Jack an emphatic nod.

"Okay," said Jack, coming over to us, "let's have a look at some charts, Hotwire."

Phil went to a cabinet and found maps of the city sewers. I located the main sewer I'd walked along when I escaped from Mouseman's control center.

"Now," said Phil, "where did you come out after crawling along the duct? This is important because if you can give us an idea of the direction you took, we won't raid the wrong house. If Mouseman even catches a hint that we're on to him, he'll do something drastic."

"I dropped out of the duct on this side of the sewer tunnel, right about here," I said, pointing. "It came in at right angles."

"How long did you crawl?" asked Jack, and I told him. "Right," he said, taking out a stopwatch. "Now, I want you to crawl down the corridor at the same speed you used when you escaped through the duct."

I was a bit worried. "I can't remember how fast I crawled."

"Just close your eyes and imagine you're still in the duct, with all the dust and spiders around you. You'll remember. You said you moved along on your knees; do the same thing now. I'm going to time you over a ten-meter stretch."

Blindboy said, "You can do it, Hotwire."

So we went out into the corridor and I hunched myself against the wall, closed my eyes, and began to crawl. My knees and elbows were still sore from last time. I tried to imagine I was still in the duct, the way Jack had said, and it seemed to work. I really felt I was there. Finally I bumped my head against the end wall and opened my eyes. Jack was looking at the stopwatch.

"Okay," he said, "you crawled ten meters in three minutes, so in thirty minutes you would have traveled ten times that distance."

"One hundred meters," said Blindboy.

We went back into the office.

"Right," said Phil, looking at the big chart again. He began to trace along the map with his finger. Then he went over to a computer and punched some keys. Finally he looked up. "That puts us," he said, "at Walsam House."

"What's Walsam House?" I asked.

"Big mansion, by the look of it. Used to be owned by a banker until he shot himself," said Jack.

"Or someone shot him," muttered Blindboy.

The two policemen stared at Blindboy for a moment. "The boy could be right," said Phil. "Mouseman."

"The house I was in was certainly big," I said. "Had a long driveway and when they dragged me through it I saw a huge hall and this staircase you wouldn't believe."

Phil asked, "Anything else? Any unusual features?"

I thought hard. "Yeah," I said. "There were these two stone animals, one on either side of the steps. One was a lion"—I'd seen a picture of a lion on zoo posters—"and the other one was a kind of horse thing, with a spike coming out of its head, right here." I pointed to the middle of my forehead.

Jack grinned. "That's it! The lion and the unicorn! That mansion was built by a guy called Rochester— he had some idea he was related to English nobility.

Okay Phil, get some men together. We're going on a raid."

Suddenly great excitement filled the air as uniformed policemen and policewomen gathered downstairs. Jack said to us, "We'll be back soon."

"I want to come," I said.

"So do I," added Blindboy. "We've been in this from the start. We've got a right to see the end."

"You'd be in danger," said Jack.

I laughed at that. "What do you think I was in when I found the place? At least I'm on the right side this time."

Jack pursed his lips, then shrugged his shoulders. "Okay, but you have to stay in the bender. I don't want you getting in the way. You hear me?"

"We hear you, boss," I said, the excitement building up in me now.

So a cavalcade of benders left the station, driving toward the edge of the city. I could feel Blindboy trembling in anticipation beside me. I grabbed his hand and held it for a while. He didn't seem to mind.

When we reached the driveway we swept up it at full speed and skidded to a halt outside the doors. Then policemen were everywhere. We heard shots from somewhere behind the house and Phil told us to duck down, but I didn't want to miss a thing.

Once the house doors were opened, Jack and Phil jumped out of their bender and went running up the

129

steps, then vanished inside. I saw a policewoman frog-marching Joe the gorilla down the marble steps. She took him to a wazzoovan with bars at the window and pushed him inside. Other members of the gang were trying to escape by jumping from windows and running across the lawns, but the cops had all the exits covered and I doubt anyone got through them.

"What's happening?" Blindboy kept yelling, and I had to keep up a running description of everything that went on around us.

Suddenly Jack came out, bounded down the steps, and ran over to us. "Quick," he said, "Hotwire. Come show us the trigger to the secret door—the one you told us was in the cellar that leads to Mouseman's computer control center. We can't find it."

I leaped out of the bender and followed Jack into the house.

I was hustled into the cellar, where I went straight to the part of the wall where I saw them press the wet stone. After three tries I found the right one and the wine vat tipped up, revealing the steps to the control center.

Jack, Phil, the other policemen, and I went racing down the stairs. I'd come this far and I wasn't going to miss what happened next. When we got to the bottom of the stairs, white-coated technicians were running everywhere. Police grabbed them as they ran past. There was really nowhere to go. In making his fortress secure, Mouseman had left no way of escape.

One technician with goofy teeth tried to run past me but was grabbed by a policeman and hauled in front of Jack.

"Hello, Tweedle," I said.

Tweedle looked down at me, his eyes wide with fright. "You!" he said.

"Where's Mouseman?" asked Jack.

Tweedle stared at him, his eyes still bugging.

"You'd better tell Jack where he is," I said. "If you do, Jack will put in a word for you at your trial, won't you, Jack?"

"Will I?" said Jack. "Yes, I suppose I will."

"He's back there," said Tweedle, swallowing quickly, then pointing nervously toward the middle of the computer center. "He's going to blow up the city."

Jack thrust Tweedle into the arms of a cop and ran down the corridor to where two policewomen were confronting a little man whose hand was on a red lever. Jack pulled up short. Phil came a second later. I stood between them.

"Don't come any closer," screamed Mouseman. "I have bombs under every government building in the city. If I pull this lever you'll be responsible for thousands of deaths. . . ."

"*We'll* be responsible," said Phil. "That's rich!"

"Just don't come any closer," Mouseman snarled. There were beads of sweat on his face and his eyes were wild. "I'll blow you all to pieces!"

A huge crowd of police were gathered now, confronting Mouseman, whose white knuckles showed how serious he was about pulling the lever.

Jack said quietly, "Okay, everybody, let's just keep calm. I want you all to move back toward the stairs. We don't want to upset Mr. Mouseman here, do we? And you, Mouseman, you be careful with that lever."

The sweat was pouring from Mouseman's face now—and from one or two others', including Jack's. Mouseman gave a kind of sneering smile as the police gradually began to withdraw. "That's better," he grunted. "I'm still the boss around here, the man with the brains."

"No you're not!" I yelled, and made a rush for him. "I've got a few brains too!"

Jack shouted something and tried to grab me, but I'd had enough of this loudmouthed coward. It was time to show him that he couldn't push people around. The last thing I heard before Mouseman pulled the lever was Phil's frightened yell that the girl was *crazy*.

I heard the horrified gasps of the cops behind me as the lever came down. Then I butted Mouseman in the stomach until he fell to the floor, gasping and groaning.

What happened next was everyone got soaked as the fire-prevention sprinkler system came on. Water showered from the ceiling and hissed and spurted from nozzles in the wall. We all got a thorough drenching.

Mouseman was immediately seized by two cops who dragged him away kicking and screaming.

Jack grabbed hold of me. "I don't understand," he said through the downpour, water running from his hat in rivulets. "What's happened here? I haven't heard any explosions."

"You won't," I told him. "When I was a prisoner down here I opened the panel to the bomb computer and changed all the wires. I rewired the bomb signals to activate the sprinkler systems instead. That's why you're wet."

"Hotwire," he said, "you're a genius." Jack smiled at me through the rain.

"I know, but I can't help it," I answered, smiling back. "Me and Blindboy, we're the last two geniuses left."

Blindboy was waiting for us in the bender, and when I described what had happened he hooted with laughter and slapped me on the back. I had to tell him the story several times as we drove back to Jack's place. There Phil shook our hands.

"I was wrong about you two," he said seriously, "right from the start."

"That's okay," said Blindboy. "We can live with a few mistakes."

Phil smiled and said, "Thanks—for everything."

When we entered Jack's apartment Barb was there, and she quickly produced towels for Jack and me. We dried off, and then all of us sat down to a steaming supper of good wholesome food and hot cocoa. But Blindboy and me didn't mind that—we intended getting some burgers at the first opportunity, and some Frizzo to go with them.

Later Jack said to us, "I promised to do something for you and I will. Tomorrow. Tonight you sleep here."

The following morning he took us to The Golden Arcade, the place of many computer shops. There he spoke a long time to an elderly Chinese man called John Woo, who finally beckoned us forward with a smile.

"Mr. Rickman tells me you are good with computers," said John Woo.

We both nodded. "Pretty good," said Blindboy.

"What I need," said John Woo, "is two good technicians. My eyes are failing me now. I need some young eyes."

"Can't help you there," said Blindboy cheerfully. "I haven't got any eyes to spare. But I'm good with my hands. I've got young hands and I can feel my way through any problem."

"He can hear ultrasonic sounds," I remarked to John Woo. "He can tell whether a circuit's live or not."

"That could prove most useful," said John Woo, nodding his head slowly. "When can you both start work?"

"Yesterday?" I said.

We all laughed.

o——o

So now Blindboy and me work for John Woo at The Golden Arcade. John Woo is too old to be a father to us, but he's kind of like a grandfather, and Celia Woo, his wife, is even more like a grandma. They treat us like real kids and yell at us if we're doing something bad, give us chores to do around the house, and give us treats sometimes too. They don't moon over us or do any of that mushy stuff, but we all eat together at one table and Celia makes us mind our manners. They talk to us and listen to what we have to say too, as if it's just as important as what ordinary people say.

I tell Blindboy this is like a real family acts and he just smiles that weird smile of his and shakes his head, not saying no, but probably thinking, Yeah, brother and sister.

We do good business too. The dump kids come in to see us with computer parts and we give them a good price. They don't go to anyone else, because they know we'll treat them fairly. That's all most of them ask for.

Blindboy is still blind of course, but there is a faint hope that one day he might be able to see. We've been working on this swazz electronic device that skips the eyes altogether and feeds images directly to the brain. It's a kind of sensor unit that picks out shapes of objects around the person who's using it. It's not *seeing* exactly, this world of shadows, but it's better than being totally blind. All we need now is the money for a surgeon to implant the device in Blindboy's head and we're saving up for that.

No one treats us like slummers anymore. We're sort of the same kids we always were, but there's a difference too. I used to think Blindboy needed me to look after him, but somehow he seems more sure of himself now. He needs me, but not to look after him, just to be there. After all, we're family.

And me? I'm kind of changed inside too—and outside also, I guess. Jack Rickman says I'm turning into a real lady, which he knows makes me mad, but even though I yell at him to stop kidding me I feel good inside. There's a kind of admiration in his voice that makes me feel proud of myself.

Whenever John Woo gets a customer he wants to

impress, he points to us working in the back of the shop. "That one's Blindboy and she's Hotwire," he says. "Between them they brought down the whole Mouseman empire."

And the customer stares, sees two young kids busy fiddling with computer parts, and goes away shaking his head and laughing at John Woo's famous joke.